PORTRAITS
of LITTLE WOMEN
*Birthday
Wishes*

Don't miss any of the
Portraits of Little Women

PORTRAITS of LITTLE WOMEN

Birthday Wishes

Four Stories

Susan Beth Pfeffer

DELACORTE PRESS

Published by
Delacorte Press
a division of Random House, Inc.
1540 Broadway
New York, New York 10036

Library of Congress Cataloging-in-Publication Data
Cataloging-in-Publication Data is available from the Library of Congress.

ISBN: 0-385-32709-9

The text of this book is set in 13-point Cochin.

Book design by Patrice Sheridan

Cover illustration © 1999 by Lori Earley
Text illustrations © 1999 by Marcy Ramsey
Recipe illustrations © 1999 by Laura Maestro

Manufactured in the United States of America

November 1999

10 9 8 7 6 5 4 3 2 1

BVG

TO ESTHER AND ALAN PFEFFER, WHO SHARE
TWO LIVES
AND ONE BIRTHDAY

CONTENTS

Meg's Birthday Wish

CHAPTER 1

"Meg," Marmee said, "would you run an errand for me?"

"Of course, Marmee," Meg replied. It was a lovely spring day, and Meg March could think of nothing better than to have an excuse to leave her schoolbooks and go outside.

"I just realized we're low on flour," Marmee said. "And Hannah wants to bake some bread for tomorrow. Could you go to the grocer and pick some up?"

"How much do you need?" Meg asked. She felt especially good that Marmee had asked such a favor of her, for in just a few days, Meg was going to celebrate her tenth birthday. She was growing up, and Marmee was now trusting her to run errands on her own.

"Five pounds," Marmee replied. "If you think you can manage that much."

"I'll go with her," Jo volunteered. "Then Meg can carry half and I can carry the other half."

"Could I go too?" Beth asked. "Then Meg and Jo wouldn't have to carry nearly so much."

"I want to go as well," Amy said.

Marmee smiled at her daughters. "What good girls you are to offer to help your big sister."

"Does that mean we can go?" Jo asked.

"It certainly does," Marmee replied. "Meg, keep an eye on your sisters. Make sure you all hold hands, and be careful if any horses and carriages go by."

"Yes, Marmee," Meg said. She couldn't explain why, but she no longer felt excited.

Marmee got out her purse, found some coins, and began to hand them to Meg.

"I want to hold the money!" Amy cried. "Please!"

"Very well then," Marmee said. "But you must be very careful with it, Amy. We can't afford to lose even a penny if we're to have bread tomorrow."

"I'll be careful," Amy declared. "I'm a big girl."

Jo laughed, and even Beth smiled. Only Meg wasn't amused. If Amy, the youngest of her sisters, held the money, and each of them pitched in to carry the flour, it didn't matter that she was almost ten and the one Marmee had singled out to run the errand.

Marmee dug through her purse again. "What do we have here?" she said. "Four pennies. One for each of you to buy some candy."

"Thank you, Marmee!" Jo shouted.

"There's no need to yell," Meg said. "Thank you, Marmee." She tried very hard to sound like a lady, but her voice was so low, she was sure Marmee couldn't hear her over Beth's and Amy's squeals of excitement.

"Be careful, girls," Marmee said as Meg left

5

the house, followed by her three younger sisters. "Don't forget to hold hands."

"We won't," Meg promised. "Jo, take Amy's hand. Beth, you walk with me."

"I want to walk with you," Jo said. "Not with Amy. I want to tell you an idea I had for a story."

"I want to walk with Meg too," Amy said.

"Then, Jo, you take my left hand, and, Amy, you take my right," Meg said.

"Whose hand should I hold?" Beth asked.

"Jo's," Meg said, but then she realized they'd be walking in a horizontal line, with Beth near the middle of the road. "That won't do at all," she said. "Jo, take Amy's hand. Beth, you walk with me."

"I don't want to walk with Jo!" Amy cried. "She walks too fast. I want to walk with you."

"Meg walks faster than I do," Jo said. "She's taller, and her legs are longer."

"But you run everywhere," Amy whined. "I want to walk with Meg."

Meg sighed. "Amy, take my hand. Jo, you and Beth walk together."

"But Bethy always walks so slowly," Jo grumbled. "And I do like to run. Why can't Beth and Amy both walk with you, Meg, and I'll run on ahead."

"Because Marmee said we were to walk together, holding hands," Meg said.

"I'm sorry I walk so slowly," Beth said. "I'll try to speed up, Jo. I'll even run."

"It's hard to run holding hands," Jo replied.

Meg realized they had scarcely walked ten feet from their house. She caught a glimpse of Marmee looking out the window, undoubtedly wondering what was keeping them from going into town.

"We have an errand to run," Meg said. "We're getting nowhere standing around fighting over who holds whose hand. Jo, take Amy's hand. Beth, you walk with me."

"If I have to walk with Jo, I'm not going," Amy said.

"Fine. Stay home." Meg held out her hands. "Come, girls. Beth, take my left hand, and, Jo, my right."

The girls headed off. They had walked just a few feet when Jo stopped.

"What is it now?" Meg asked.

"Amy has the money," said Jo.

Beth burst out laughing. "Oh, Meg," she said. "If you could just see the look on your face."

Meg had no desire to see how she looked. "Amy!" she called, turning around. "Please give us the money."

"No," shouted Amy. "If I do, you'll buy all the candy for yourselves and not bring me any."

"Then come along with us," Jo said. "And buy your own candy."

"Only if I can walk with Meg," Amy replied.

"Jo, walk with Beth," Meg said. "Amy, walk with me. But please, let's get going."

"All right," Jo grumbled. "But I thought this walk was going to be fun."

Meg had thought so too. But that was before her little sisters had decided to tag along.

CHAPTER 2

Almost as soon as Meg and Jo got home from school the next day, it began to rain. Jo grumbled because she had wanted to play hoops outdoors, but Meg didn't mind the rain. She enjoyed hearing it fall onto their roof, and the cozy way it made her feel to be home and dry.

After they had dropped off their things in their bedroom, Jo decided to stay and read a book. Meg headed downstairs but peeked in on Beth and Amy and smiled when she saw them playing with their dolls.

Making her way into the parlor, Meg found Marmee sitting by the fire, patching a dress for Beth. The clothes Meg wore were handed down to her sisters one by one. Meg took special care to keep her dresses looking as new as possible for Jo, but by the time Jo was ready to hand them down to Beth, they were heavily patched.

"I'll help you with your mending, Marmee," Meg offered. "It's the perfect weather for that."

"How very nice, dear," Marmee replied.

She smiled as Meg picked up a needle and thread and began sewing a hem on a dress she was handing down to Jo. "Jo is so rough on her clothes," Marmee said. "It's all right now, while Beth is still at home. But next year she'll be in school, and she'll need decent clothing."

"I could go without a new dress for a year," Meg offered. "That way you could take the material you just bought and make a dress for Beth."

"That's very kind of you," Marmee said. "I'm hoping it won't be necessary, though. Aunt March might give us some money to celebrate Beth's first year of school."

Meg knew her family depended on Aunt March's generosity. Meg's father was a minister, and what little extra money he made always seemed to go to people whose needs were greater than theirs.

"Aunt March can be very nice at times," Meg said.

Marmee nodded. "She means well. She just doesn't always agree with your father about what is important in life."

Meg felt very mature being told such a thing. She could think of nothing more pleasant than to be sitting by the fire, sewing with her mother.

"Marmee!" came a shout from upstairs.

"Yes, Amy, what is it?"

"I'm bored!"

"Then come down and keep us company," Marmee replied.

Meg sighed. Her mother certainly wouldn't continue to discuss Aunt March with her now.

Amy ran into the parlor and practically leaped into her mother's lap. "Tell me a story," she demanded.

Marmee laughed. "I'm not the storyteller in this family. Jo is. You should ask her for a story."

"Jo!" Amy shouted. "Come downstairs!"

Jo appeared seconds later. "What is it?" she asked. "Is everything all right?"

"Marmee says you're to tell us a story," Amy said. "Right now."

"Oh," Jo said. "Well, if Marmee says I should, then I will."

"May I come downstairs too?" they heard Beth ask from the second-floor landing.

"Of course, dearest," Marmee said. "Come right down, and Jo will entertain us all with one of her wonderful stories."

"One with princes and princesses," Amy said. "They're my favorites. When I grow up, I want to be a princess."

"There aren't any princesses in the United States," Meg said, feeling annoyed that her quiet time with Marmee had been interrupted.

"Then I shall go to Europe," Amy said so loftily that Marmee burst out laughing.

"I'll miss you if you do," Marmee said. "But,

Jo, favor us with a story of princes and princesses if you would."

"I'd be delighted." Jo plopped herself by the fire, with little regard to the damage she might do to her dress. Beth sat down by Marmee's side, and Amy continued to cuddle on Marmee's lap.

"This is so lovely," Marmee said. "To have all my daughters with me on this drizzly, gray day."

Meg didn't think things were nearly as lovely as they had been just a few minutes earlier. How was she ever to learn interesting things about Aunt March and Father if she was constantly surrounded by little sisters?

"Once upon a time there was a beautiful princess," Jo began.

"Did she have blond curls like me?" Amy asked.

"She did," Jo said, which Meg knew meant Jo was in a good mood. Otherwise, she would have given her princess raven hair, just to annoy Amy.

"Did she have any sisters?" Meg asked.

"None," Jo replied.

"Poor thing," Beth said. "I should be so lonely if I didn't have any sisters."

"Perhaps the princess had a brother," Marmee suggested.

"No brothers either," said Jo. "The princess was all alone in the world."

"How sad," said Beth.

All alone, Meg thought. No whiny, pesky little sisters tagging along, making demands, taking time away from her and Marmee. She smiled at the thought.

"Meg is enjoying your story already," Marmee said.

"It's a wonderful story," Meg said, but what was truly wonderful was the idea brewing in her head.

CHAPTER 3

After Meg and Jo had gone to bed that night, Meg listened for the sound of her sister's deep and steady breathing. Once she was certain Jo was asleep, she crept out of bed, put on her slippers, and tiptoed downstairs. She found her parents sitting by the parlor fire, talking in quiet voices.

"Meg!" Marmee said, obviously startled. "Are you feeling all right?"

"Yes, I'm fine," Meg said. "I just wanted to talk to you."

"You need your sleep," Father said. "Tomorrow is a school day."

"I won't stay up long," Meg said. "I promise."

"It must be important," Marmee said. "What do you want to talk about?"

"My birthday," Meg replied. "It's on Saturday."

"We know," Father said, smiling. "But if you've come to find out what your birthday present is, you might as well go back to bed. You'll be unwrapping it soon enough."

"I know I'll love my present, no matter what it is," Meg said. "But there's something else I'd like."

"A party?" Marmee asked. "You didn't want one a few weeks ago, and there isn't much time to prepare for one now. But I'm sure Hannah and I could arrange something if you want to invite a few friends over."

"No, that isn't it at all," Meg said, knowing that if she had a party, her sisters would insist on attending. "What I want most for my birthday is some time alone with you. Both of you."

Father looked puzzled. "Time alone?" he asked.

Meg nodded. "I never have any time alone with you," she said, trying hard not to whine. "I just want a day without sisters."

"I see. Well, I think it could be arranged," Marmee said. "Hannah could take Beth and Jo and Amy to Aunt March's for the day."

"Your sisters love you very much," Father said.

"Meg knows that," Marmee replied. "And we both know how much she loves them. But I can see that for one day it would be fun not to have the responsibility of caring for three little sisters. And I think it would be delightful to have a chance to spend some time alone with my firstborn."

"Perhaps it might be best to surprise Aunt March," said Father. "She might leave the country if she's warned in advance."

Marmee laughed. "We'll have to take that chance, I'm afraid. I was going to call on Aunt March tomorrow anyway. I'll tell her about the visit, and I'll give strict instructions to the girls to behave themselves."

"I'm sure they'll be fine," Meg said. "Aunt March loves to fuss over Amy, and Jo and Beth can entertain each other."

"It sounds as though you've thought this all out," Father said. "I hadn't realized that your sisters wearied you so."

"Three little sisters could weary a saint sometimes," Marmee said. "Go back to bed, Meg. I'll arrange everything with Aunt March, and you'll have your birthday wish for time alone with Father and me. I promise you."

"Thank you, Marmee," Meg said. She kissed both her parents, and made her way back to her room. As she climbed into bed, she looked over at her sleeping sister. Jo's beautiful long hair was loose on her pillow, and her peaceful breathing made her look angelic. Suddenly Meg felt a pang of guilt, for she knew Jo hated having to spend time with Aunt March.

But I have rights too, Meg thought. It wasn't as though she was requesting that her sisters move in with Aunt March. But just once, for a special event like her tenth birthday, Meg felt entitled to some special quiet time with her parents.

And knowing her parents agreed helped her fall asleep all the sooner.

C H A P T E R 4

" I don't see why we have to go visit Aunt March," Jo grumbled on Saturday morning.

"Because that's Meg's birthday wish," Marmee explained for the hundredth time by Meg's count.

"But I thought Meg loved us," Amy said.

"She does," Marmee said. "Don't you, Meg?"

"I love you, Amy," Meg said. "I love all of you. And if you love me, you'll visit Aunt March, without complaining."

"I'm not complaining," Beth said. "But I

was looking forward to spending your birth-day with you."

"And you will tonight," Meg said. "You're just going off for the day." She sighed. It wasn't fair. Her one birthday wish, and she was made to feel guilty about it.

"Come, girls," Marmee said. "It will be nice for you to visit Aunt March. You can play in her garden and look at all the pretty things she brought back from her last trip to Europe. Hannah?"

"I'm coming," Hannah said. "Let's get go-ing. The sooner there, the sooner home."

"Not soon enough," Jo mumbled, but if Marmee heard her, she didn't say anything. Instead she kissed each of her three younger daughters and watched as they began the walk to Aunt March's house.

"Are they holding hands?" Meg asked, re-luctant to watch as they disappeared down the street.

Marmee nodded. "Hannah is holding on to Beth and Amy," she said. "Jo is running ahead of them. I'm sure they'll all be fine."

"You don't mind, do you?" Meg asked. "Am I being horribly selfish?"

"Not at all," Marmee replied. She stroked Meg's hair. "Your father and I both like having time with you alone. I try to give each of my daughters individual attention, but it's not easy. With you and Jo at school, I know I spend far more hours with Beth and Amy. That means I try to enjoy the things you and I share together all the more." She smiled. "It seems to me we were interrupted during our mending. Would you enjoy picking up where we left off?"

"I'd like that," Meg said. She got her bag of mending and joined Marmee on the parlor sofa. There was no need for a fire on such a warm spring day. "Will Father be joining us?"

"He's going to work through lunch on his sermon for tomorrow," Marmee said. "Then this afternoon he's taking you on a long walk."

"Oh, how nice," Meg said. She couldn't remember the last time she'd taken a walk alone with Father.

"So, tell me about school," Marmee said, as she started stitching. "Are you enjoying your classes?"

Meg shrugged. "School's all right," she said. "Did you like school when you were ten?"

"Most of the time." Marmee laughed. "But it wasn't my favorite topic on my tenth birthday!"

Meg laughed too. "Do you remember your tenth birthday?" she asked.

Marmee nodded. "I had a birthday party," she said. "Quite a fancy one."

"Did you have lots and lots of money when you were ten?" Meg asked.

"I suppose I did," Marmee said. "My family certainly was comfortable. We lacked for nothing."

"That must have been wonderful," Meg said.

"It was," Marmee replied. "But I prefer the way our family lives. My parents traveled, and I didn't see much of them. I remember feeling lonely as a child. Even on my tenth birthday, my parents were in New York. They brought me back many pretty presents, but what I really wanted was to be with them."

"I'm sorry," Meg said. It was hard to picture her mother as a lonely young girl, and she hated the thought that Marmee had ever been unhappy.

Marmee smiled. "The important thing is that I met your father and we fell in love," she said. "Together we made a beautiful family — Aunt March and all. I hope my daughters meet and marry men as wonderful as your father. Especially you."

"Me?" Meg asked, putting down her mending. "Why?"

"I suppose it's because, of all my daughters, you resemble me the most," Marmee said. "Every time I see you playing with or watching over your sisters, I can't help seeing you with children of your own. Of course, that won't be for many years, but when it happens, I know you're going to be a loving mother."

"The way you are," Meg said.

"The way I try to be," said Marmee. "Sometimes my temper gets the best of me, the way it does with Jo. And sometimes I want to hide from life, the way Bethy does. And sometimes I want to have my own way, and I behave no better than Amy. I see myself in all my daughters, and I wish for them to have only what I know to be good in me, and none of my bad traits."

"You have no bad traits," Meg declared. "You're the best mother in the world."

"You're a dear to say that," Marmee said. "But we all have a long way to go before we reach perfection."

Meg considered how far that meant for her, and decided to think about it sometime other than her birthday. Marmee must have had the same thought, because she burst out laughing. "How serious we are," she said. "And on such a pretty day."

There was a knock at the front door. "Meg, dearest, would you answer that? My arms are full with this dress."

Meg got up and walked to the door. When

she opened it, she saw Mrs. James, who lived down the road.

"Hello, Meg," Mrs. James said. "Is your mother in? I need to speak to her."

"I'm in the parlor," Marmee called out, but by the time Meg and Mrs. James got there, she was already standing up, the dress neatly folded and resting on the couch.

"I'm sorry to bother you, Mrs. March," Mrs. James said. "But little Henry is running a terrible fever, and I sent my husband to find the doctor, only to learn he's gone to Lexington. You're so good with sick children. If it's not too much trouble, do you think you could come and see what you can do for Henry?"

"Of course," Marmee said. "Just give me a moment to get my things." She paused, then turned to Meg. "Dearest, you do understand?" she said. "I'll be back as soon as I possibly can."

Meg swallowed her disappointment. "Take care of Henry," she said. "And let me know if there's anything I can do to help."

Marmee smiled. "I'm sure Henry will be

fine." She put on a light coat and gathered her purse. "Tell your father where I've gone." Nodding, Meg let her mother give her a quick kiss, and she watched as Marmee followed Mrs. James out of the house.

CHAPTER 5

*M*eg knocked on Father's door. "Father?" she asked. "May I come in?"

"By all means," Father said. "What is it, Meg?"

"Marmee asked me to tell you she's gone to help Mrs. James," Meg replied. "Little Henry has a fever, and Mrs. James is worried about him."

"The boy has been sickly," Father said, nodding. "I'm not surprised Mrs. James turned to your mother for help."

"Are you working on your sermon?" Meg asked.

"As a matter of fact, I am."

"Then I'll leave you alone."

"No," Father said. "I'll just put my work away for a while. It's your birthday, after all, and you shouldn't be by yourself."

"Marmee said you were going to take me on a walk," Meg said. "After lunch."

"There's no law that says we can't take our walk before lunch," Father said. "In fact, it will help me concentrate better if I've had a chance to enjoy some fresh air with my daughter. Come, Meg, let's go for our stroll now."

"Are you sure?"

"Of course," Father replied. "I've been looking forward to our walk." He put down his pen, blotted his manuscript, and got up with a stretch. "Let's stroll toward Mr. Emerson's house," he said. "I have a question I want to ask him, and I'm sure he'd be delighted to wish you a happy birthday."

Meg had no objection to seeing Mr. Emerson, her favorite of her father's friends. And she was very pleased when her father took her by the hand as they headed outside.

"I wasn't quite sure what tomorrow's sermon would be about until you made your birthday wish," Father said. "You inspired me, you know."

"I did?" Meg asked.

Father nodded. "I'm writing about simple pleasures. How sometimes we feel as though we must have things, and yet more things, when what we really want is just some quiet time for ourselves."

"Do you feel that way too?" Meg asked.

"Frequently," Father answered. "The world is such a busy place. When I was a boy, there was no telegraph, no photography, no railroads. A trip to New York was an unimaginable journey, and now it's something that can be achieved in a day."

"But those changes are good," Meg said. "Aren't they?"

"I think they are," Father said. "And I look forward to even greater changes. I look forward to seeing this country free of the wretched misery of slavery. And I think that must happen, not simply because slavery is evil, but because there are going to be innumerable changes in the way all people live. I believe this century, the nineteenth century, will be one of enormous progress." He stopped for a moment, then laughed. "I seem to be writing my sermon as we speak," he said. "And I'm telling you about the future. Think of it, Meg. You'll live to see the twentieth century. What marvels will exist by then."

"I'll be an old lady," Meg said. "As old as Aunt March!"

"Now, there's a terrifying thought," Father said. "My little Meg as old as Aunt March."

Meg tried to picture herself decades from now. Then she tried to picture Aunt March as a ten-year-old and found that an even more terrifying thought.

"I wonder what the twentieth century will be like," Meg said. "Do you think everybody will be free, the world over?"

"I hope so," Father replied. "And I hope all people in this country will have the vote. Women as well as men, and people of all races and incomes. Then we'd truly be living up to the promise of the Declaration of Independence."

Meg couldn't remember her father's ever talking to her as though she were an adult.

"One thing I'm certain of," Father continued. "People forty-five years from now will be reading the works of Mr. Emerson just as they do today."

"And Jo's works as well," Meg said.

Father nodded. "And Jo's as well."

They walked in companionable silence the rest of the way to Mr. Emerson's. When they arrived, Mr. Emerson was standing by the front door.

"I saw you coming," he said as he greeted them. "Happy birthday, Meg. How does it feel to be ten?"

"I like it," Meg said with a smile. "I don't ever want to go back to being nine."

Mr. Emerson and Father both laughed. "A good thing too," Mr. Emerson said. "It's always harder to travel back to the past than ahead to the future."

"That's what Meg and I were talking about on our walk," Father said. "The future and all it has to offer."

"I'm afraid what the immediate future has to offer is a problem I must discuss with you," Mr. Emerson said. "I just received a telegraph from the Reverend Beecher about what is happening in Kansas. I hate to take your father from you, Meg, on your birthday, but this really is quite important."

"I understand," Meg said. There were terrible problems in Kansas that had to do with slavery, and she knew how concerned her father was about them. "Father, I'll go home by myself. Don't worry about me."

"Thank you, Meg," Father said. "I promise I'll be home very shortly."

Meg nodded. She said good-bye to her father and to Mr. Emerson and began the solitary walk home.

When Meg arrived home, Marmee had not yet returned, but Hannah was in the kitchen, and Meg joined her.

"Did you take my sisters to Aunt March's?" Meg asked.

"Of course I did," Hannah replied. "Amy made a fuss, and Jo sulked, and Beth acted as though the world was about to end, but I got them to Mrs. March's just as I was asked to. Now I'm trying to get a full day's worth of work done in half a day. So if you want any sort of fancy dinner and cake for your birthday, I suggest you stay out of my way and let me get to it."

"Can't I help?" Meg asked.

"On your birthday? Certainly not. Go enjoy yourself, and let me work."

Meg left the kitchen. The house seemed awfully quiet, even with Hannah in the kitchen. Meg had wanted time away from her sisters, but she had never imagined feeling quite so lonely.

Going back into the parlor, she picked up her mending. She never minded sewing, but she was accustomed to having her sisters chattering nearby and her mother working along with her. Even if her father was busy in his study, it comforted her to know he was there. Today she was all alone.

Meg left her mending and went upstairs. First she looked into Beth and Amy's room. The girls kept it neat, with their dolls lined up by their beds. Amy loved to draw, and her table was filled with her pretty little pictures. Meg picked one up and realized it was of her and her sisters. "Happy Birthday, Meg," Amy had written in her childish printing.

Meg realized the picture was supposed to be a surprise, Amy's special gift to her. She quickly left the room and went to the one she shared with Jo.

Jo wasn't as neat, but even she made an effort to keep things tidy. The weather was already warm enough for Jo to do her scribblings in the attic, so their table wasn't as cluttered as Beth and Amy's.

Meg knew there had been a time when her family consisted of only Father, Marmee, and herself—a time before Jo had been born—but she couldn't remember it. It seemed that all Meg's life, Jo had been by her side, inventing games, telling stories, laughing and fighting and making her presence felt even as she slept. It just didn't seem right to be in the room without her, even if it was Meg's bedroom every bit as much as it was Jo's.

Nothing in the house felt right without her

sisters. Meg suddenly regretted having sent them into exile at Aunt March's.

Going downstairs, Meg returned to the parlor. She knew she should pick up her mending, but she had no desire to. She walked to the front window and stared out. Soon she was rewarded by the sight of Marmee walking toward the house.

Meg raced out the front door. "How is Henry?" she asked.

"Better, I think," Marmee replied. "His fever is down, and Mrs. James seems less worried, so I decided to come home."

"I'm glad you did," Meg said. "Father is at Mr. Emerson's, and I missed you both."

"I'm sorry, dear," Marmee said. "But I'm back now, and we can return to our conversation if you like."

"Perhaps some other time," Meg said. "Marmee, would you think it terrible of me if I went to Aunt March's and brought everyone back?"

Marmee smiled. "By all means, fetch your sisters," she said. "I don't think Aunt March would object at all to the visit's being cut short."

"We'll be back as soon as possible," Meg said.

"Just be careful," Marmee said. "Make sure you all hold hands, and watch out—"

"—for horses and carriages," Meg said, with a laugh. "I promise we will." She waved good-bye, and walked as swiftly as she felt a lady should to Aunt March's.

When she arrived, she found her sisters sitting in abject misery in Aunt March's back parlor. "Oh, Meg!" Jo cried. "Have you come to rescue us?"

"Jo," Meg whispered. "What if Aunt March hears you?"

"She escaped to her bedroom an hour ago," Jo said. "She told us to sit here and not make a sound."

"She said we gave her a headache," Beth said.

"Even me," Amy said. "And she likes me."

Meg laughed. "I'm sorry. I'll never desert you again. Now let's go home and play together, and make lots of lovely noise in honor of my birthday."

"I want to hold your hand," Amy said. "Jo squeezes too hard when I walk with her."

"I want to walk with Meg," Jo said. "It's my right because I'm older than you are, Amy, and it's Meg's birthday."

"I'd like to walk with Meg too," Beth said.

Meg looked at each of her sisters and realized they really did all want to walk with her—and that was very nice indeed. "We'll take turns," she said. "Because I'd like to walk with each one of you as well. I'll start with Amy, because she's the youngest, and then Beth, and then you, Jo."

"I'll keep time, to make sure we all share your company equally," Jo said. "Starting right now."

"Come, Amy," Meg said. She reached down and took Amy's hand. Beth and Jo locked arms, and after telling Aunt March's butler to give her their thanks and good-byes, the girls hurried outside.

One by one they began to chatter, until Meg

was sure there had never been four noisier girls in the world. And even though her birthday wish had been to have time away from her younger sisters, Meg felt blessed to have them share in the celebration of her tenth birthday—and most of all she loved the fact that she was one of the four.

Jo's
Birthday
Wish

CHAPTER 1

"Josephine! Josephine March!"

"Yes, Aunt March?"

"Stop what you are doing and come here at once."

Jo sighed. There was no arguing with Aunt March, especially when that tone crept into her voice. Jo put down the shovel she'd been using and walked back into the house. She couldn't imagine how Aunt March had seen what she'd been up to, but Aunt March always seemed to have an instinct for catching Jo in mischief.

"You should look at yourself, Josephine,"

Aunt March scolded. "You're covered with dirt. Whatever have you been doing?"

"It's a long story," Jo said.

Aunt March rolled her eyes. "You may spare me the details," she said. "I'm sure I'll be able to imagine them anyway."

Jo wasn't sure where to begin. "I was sitting in the parlor, reading," she said. "Well, actually I was thinking more than reading. I was thinking about my birthday. It's in just a few days, you know, and I'll be ten, and I was thinking about being ten, and how that would be different from being nine."

"You are not sparing me the details," Aunt March said. "I simply want to know how you managed to get yourself covered in dirt when I left you for only a few minutes to sit in the parlor and read."

"That's what I'm trying to explain," Jo replied, wishing she didn't have to explain anything, wishing Marmee hadn't insisted she pay a call on Aunt March that afternoon. "If I'd been reading, I wouldn't have noticed the cat in your yard, and how it was chasing a baby rabbit."

"A rabbit?" said Aunt March.

"Yes. The cat chased the rabbit into your cellar. And I was certain you wouldn't care for that, so I went down after them, and we all ran around, and I bumped into a few things, and so did the rabbit, but I don't think the cat did. Then I heard some fiercesome noises, and I bumped into a few more things. Your cellar is very dark, Aunt March, and the cat saw me and bounded out. When I looked down, there was the poor little rabbit. Dead. I suppose the cat killed it."

"How very sad," Aunt March remarked, but she didn't sound very sad at all.

"That's what I thought," Jo said. "And I certainly couldn't leave the dead rabbit in your cellar, so I carried it upstairs. I was going to bring it into the woods, when I thought about how short its life had been, and I couldn't bear the thought of some owl carrying it away for breakfast tomorrow, so I decided to bury it. I wasn't going to pray over it, or give it a real funeral, because after all, it is just a rabbit, and not a very bright one at that. But it did die in your house, so I felt an obligation to it. I got the shovel and was just finished putting it in the ground when you called to me. And really, Aunt March, that is the short version."

Aunt March shook her head. "Will you never grow up?" she asked.

"I am growing up," Jo said. "Don't you remember? That's why I saw the cat in the first place, because I am growing up. Otherwise I would have been reading and you'd have a dead rabbit in your cellar."

"Dead rabbit or no dead rabbit, your face is filthy and so are your hands," Aunt March said. "In fact, your dress is so dirty, I don't know if it will ever get clean. And you've torn your sleeve. All because you didn't sit in the parlor and read, as I asked you to."

"But you really wouldn't have liked finding a dead rabbit in your cellar," Jo said.

"I don't go into my cellar," Aunt March replied. "Besides, the servants would know how to dispose of a dead animal. Without a full funeral, I am sure."

"I'm sorry," Jo said.

"There's no need to apologize to me," Aunt March answered. "I'm not the one who will have to wash your dress and try to mend it. I'm not the one who will have to wear it once you've outgrown it. Assuming the dress survives that long. Unless you broke something in my cellar, you owe me no apologies."

Jo thought back to the cellar and tried to remember if she'd heard anything crashing or smashing. She didn't think so. "If I don't owe you any apologies, why are you so angry?" she asked.

"That is a most impertinent question," Aunt March said. "Have you no manners at all, Josephine? Or are you simply a spoiled little girl?"

"I'm not spoiled, and I'm not little," Jo said. "I'm almost practically ten years old."

"Then it's about time you began behaving like a lady, and not a ragamuffin," Aunt March said. "If you're so proud of being almost practically ten, then you should stop running around, and chasing animals, and digging holes. You should be capable of sitting and reading a book."

"I am too capable!" Jo shouted. "I was only trying to do you a good deed."

"You were only looking for an excuse to run around and play in the dirt," Aunt March replied. "Go home, Josephine. I won't have you in my house covered in filth."

"I'm going," Jo mumbled. "But don't blame me if your servants find all kinds of dead creatures in your cellar someday."

"I'll be sure to remember," Aunt March responded. She walked into her house and slammed the door. Even Jo knew that meant her visit was over, and it had been none too successful a call at that.

CHAPTER 2

"Oh, Jo," Marmee said as Jo entered the house. "Whatever have you gotten yourself into this time?"

"It's a long story," Jo said. "Aunt March is so unfair."

She followed her mother into the parlor, where Meg was sitting on the sofa reading, Beth was playing on the floor with her dolls, and Amy was sketching the vase of flowers that stood on the fireplace mantel. They were all completely clean.

"Did Aunt March throw dirt at you?" Meg asked, looking up.

Jo had never felt so dirty in her life. "I

didn't mean to get covered so," she said. "But I was bumping around in Aunt March's cellar. I think that's how I tore my sleeve, and then I was digging a hole in her garden, and I guess I wasn't too careful."

Meg burst out laughing, and then her sisters joined her.

"It really isn't funny," Marmee said. "That's quite a rip in your dress, Jo. And some of these stains look as if they'll never come out."

"Then I'll be the one to suffer," Amy said. "Because someday that dress will be mine, and it's ruined already."

"Beth will have to wear it first," Meg pointed out. "And she isn't complaining."

"I'm not sure the dress will last long enough to be worn by Beth," Marmee said. "In fact, I don't know that even Jo will get much more wear out of it. I'll see if Hannah and I can get it clean enough to bother mending, but I'm not so sure."

"Oh, Marmee, I am sorry," Jo said, and this time she truly was. The March family didn't have much money for clothing, and Jo told herself over and over to be careful, since her dresses, hand-me-downs from Meg, were expected to last for Beth and Amy's use as well. When Jo got them from Meg, they seemed almost brand-new. But by the time they were ready for Beth, they were well patched.

"I'm sure you had a good reason to be in Aunt March's cellar," Marmee said. "I just wish you'd be more careful with your things."

"I will be," Jo said. "I promise."

Meg snorted.

"You make that promise a lot," Amy said.

"But Jo always means it," Beth said. "It wasn't her fault she had to go into Aunt March's cellar. I think it was very brave of Jo. Cellars scare me. I never would have gone in there."

"And you never would have ripped your dress and stained it so," Amy added. "And then it would be a much nicer dress when I have to wear it."

"As Jo gets older, I'm sure she'll become more careful," Marmee said. "Do go change, Jo, before you do the dress any further damage. And wash your face and hands. I can hardly recognize you through all that dirt."

"Yes, Marmee," Jo said. Marmee's voice was softer than Aunt March's, but Jo knew she had just been thoroughly scolded. Jo hated disappointing Marmee, and she felt miserable as she went up to her bedroom, changed out of her dress, and washed herself clean of cellar dirt. She carried the dress downstairs with extra care. "I'll wash it," she offered. "I'm the one who got it dirty, so I should be the one to get it clean."

"I think not," Marmee said. "You might do it more harm with your rough ways."

"I said I was sorry!" Jo cried. "And now you won't even let me help make things better?"

"Not if you'll only make things worse," Marmee replied. "Jo, go to your room and think about your responsibilities to yourself, to Aunt March, to your sisters, and to Hannah."

"May I go with Jo?" Beth asked. "I could help her think."

"No, this is something Jo must work out for

herself," Marmee replied. "Stay in your room, Jo, until suppertime. And then we'll talk about what you did today and what you should do in the future."

Jo knew she must have done something truly terrible to be sent to her room. She couldn't imagine what it was, though. Someone had to chase after the cat. Someone had to rescue the rabbit, even though she'd failed in the effort. And how was it wrong to bury the poor thing?

Jo climbed onto her bed and scowled. There were books to read, enough paper and ink to continue writing her current play, even a bag of mending to work on. But she knew Marmee meant for her to think, and she supposed she ought to do what Marmee had told her.

Jo sat and thought. She thought about how unfair life was: She was being punished for doing a good deed, Aunt March had been mean, and Marmee had been unjust. Her sisters, too, were unfair. Meg had laughed at her, and Amy had complained about a dress she wouldn't even wear for three years or more.

Only Beth was spared Jo's anger. Beth never complained. Beth never scolded or got angry. Beth was such a dear.

But that made Jo realize that Beth would be wearing the patched and stained dress next. Sweet Beth was the one who'd be stuck with it. It was possible that it might never make it to Amy, and so Beth, the nicest one of them all, was the one who would suffer most.

Jo tried to tell herself it was Aunt March's fault, or Marmee's, or Meg's, or even Amy's, but deep down she knew it was because of her that Beth never had a decent dress to wear. And Jo knew she didn't have to chase after rabbits or cats. Aunt March was right. Jo had run after the animals because she'd thought it would be fun to join the chase. Cats killed rabbits and owls ate rabbits, and there was nothing Jo could do to prevent nature from taking its course.

What a baby I am, Jo thought, shedding baby tears on her pillow.

CHAPTER 3

"*M*armee, may I talk to you and Father?" Jo asked after supper. No one had done much talking during the meal. Father had noticed and asked why his family was so quiet, but when Amy had tried to explain, Meg had shushed her, and Father had yet to hear the real explanation.

"Of course you may," Marmee said. "Let's talk in your father's study."

So Jo had followed her parents into her father's book-filled room. Someday Jo imagined she'd have a study where she could write her plays and stories, with no interruptions from a houseful of noisy children. Of course, she was the noisiest of the children, but even she knew to be quiet when her father was working.

"Father, I ripped my dress, and I got it hopelessly dirty," she said. "And I made Aunt March angry, and Marmee, too. And I know it's my fault, and I'm truly sorry."

"I'll have your mother tell me exactly what happened later," Father said. "I'm glad you're repentant, Jo, but sorrow isn't enough. What do you think you should do to make up for your deeds?"

"I know I'll have to write to Aunt March and apologize," Jo said. Sometimes it seemed as if she wrote more letters of apology than she did stories or plays. "And, Marmee, I'll do everything I can to fix my dress."

"I'm afraid the dress is a lost cause," Marmee said. "Hannah and I examined it very carefully, and there are stains we're sure will never come out. It's not fair to Beth to make her wear a dress in such bad condition."

"No, it isn't," Jo agreed. "So I thought if

you hadn't yet bought me any presents for my birthday, you could take the money and buy Beth a new dress."

"We'll find the money for a dress somehow," Father said. "Jo, your birthday is an important one. It's a time to celebrate, but it's also a time to think about what you want to do to be a better person. You're no longer a little girl. You're capable of making changes in yourself."

"I know that," Jo said. "I've thought about it a lot. Up to now I've run around an awful lot and played rough games. So I've decided the time has come for me to act like an adult."

Marmee smiled. "There's a difference, Jo, between ten and twenty. We don't want you to act older than you truly are."

"I have to start sometime," Jo replied. "And ten is as good a time as any. I know how fortunate I am. There are children working in factories who are younger than me, children who would starve if they didn't labor six days a week, twelve hours a day. I'm even more fortunate than Beth, since when I get my clothes from Meg, they're in fine shape. No, from now on, I'm not going to run around, or play foolish games, or do anything except complete my schoolwork, and help in the house, and be considerate of others. Including Aunt March. I want to be a daughter you'll be proud of."

"That's really quite admirable," Father said. "But truly, Jo, we won't fault you if you run around occasionally."

"All we want is for you to be more careful with your things," Marmee said.

"That's very kind of you," Jo replied. "But it isn't enough."

"You didn't mention your writing," Father said. "I hope you don't intend to give that up as well."

The thought had never crossed Jo's mind. She wondered for a moment if she ought to but then decided writing was a very grown-up thing to do. "I'll keep writing," she said. "But I'll be more careful with the ink. I'll remember to blot my manuscripts thoroughly, and I'll try not to spill any ink, or dip my sleeves in the bottle ever again."

"I must say I approve of that," Father declared. "They say the pen is mightier than the sword, and I know from my own experience, it can be messier than the sword as well."

Marmee smiled at Jo. "It sounds as though you've given this a great deal of thought," she said. "And I think we'll all be happier if you are less careless about your things. Just don't imagine we want you to be unhappy. We know how important it is for you to run around, to play outside, to explore and climb and see all that you can see. It's good for you to do those things. And while Hannah and I will both appreciate anything you do in the house to help, that's not the only way you can be useful."

"You can always help me in the garden," Father said. "That's a perfectly proper way of digging and getting dirty."

"I'll do that, I promise," Jo said. "But now that I'm almost practically ten, I'm too old to run around and climb and chase after things. I suppose if I were a boy, it would be all right, but I'm not, and it isn't, and I might as well try to be a lady now, the way Meg is always after me to be. I'll finish that sampler Aunt March gave me to work on two years ago, and I'll help Hannah with the ironing, and I'll be so good and so quiet, you'll hardly even know I'm around."

"That's what we're afraid of," Father said, but Jo assumed he was joking and merely smiled at the comment. She got up, walked over to her parents slowly and with dignity, and kissed each one gently on the cheek.

This is how a lady behaves, she told herself as she left her father's study. I'm almost practically ten now, and it's about time I behaved the way a lady does.

But somehow behaving like a lady made Jo feel a little bit like Joan of Arc marching toward the stake to be burned alive. She wondered if that was the fate of all girls who didn't want to be ladies when they grew up.

J o woke up the next morning with a start. This was the last day she'd ever be nine. The last day she'd ever be a child.

She looked over at Meg's bed and saw that her sister was still sleeping. Meg was almost twelve. She'd given up being a child a long time ago, and she didn't seem to mind.

But Jo knew things would be different for her. Meg had been born a lady. She enjoyed sitting still, playing with girls, and minding her manners. Proper behavior wasn't a struggle for her, the way it was for Jo. Meg had probably never felt like Joan of Arc.

Jo sat up in bed and thought about all she

had to do to behave like a grown-up. It wasn't going to be enough to finish a sampler. She was going to have to honor her own promise to give up running and jumping and playing in the dirt. It wasn't going to be easy.

"Christopher Columbus," she muttered at the very thought of all that she faced.

"Don't use slang," Meg mumbled as she woke up.

Jo sighed. No running, jumping, playing in the dirt, or using slang. She didn't know how ladies managed, or more to the point how *she* was going to manage.

The problem bothered her throughout the morning as she dressed and ate breakfast and prepared for school. She dawdled over the simplest tasks, and by the time she and her sisters prepared to leave, they were late, and Jo knew it was her fault.

"Come, Jo," Meg said. "If we all run, we should make it to school on time."

"You run," Jo said, yearning to. "I'll just walk fast."

Her sisters looked at her as though she'd

lost her mind, but they began to sprint. Jo forced herself to walk the way a lady would, and made it to school after the final bell had rung. Her teacher promptly instructed her to write "I will not be late to school" twenty times on the slate board, making Jo feel all the more like Joan of Arc.

When she sat down, Jo couldn't concentrate on the lesson, because it was a warm spring-time Friday. Instead she daydreamed more than normal and was scolded twice for not paying attention. When lunchtime arrived, Jo was even more miserable. All the boys ran out of the building and began racing around, shouting and tossing balls at one another. Some of the younger girls joined in the fun.

As recently as the day before, Jo would have welcomed the chance to play with the boys as an equal. She was fiercely tempted to go over to them and play as she had, telling herself she had one day left before she turned ten, one day when she could still be wild and free. But she knew that would be giving in to temptation, and she forced herself to sit still and eat lunch with Meg and her friends. She ate carefully, making sure not to spill anything on her dress. Meg's friends chattered cheerfully about parties, and clothes, and the other children in the school. It was the dreariest lunch Jo could remember.

The problem, Jo told herself after lunch, was that it was hard to behave like an adult when she was surrounded by childish things. Children behaved like children because they were treated like children, and they were treated like children because they behaved like children. Jo was stunned by this idea and would have happily shared it with her teacher, except she was supposed to be studying her spelling. Still, when she was called on to spell "considerable," she easily rattled off the correct letters. Spelling was definitely the easiest part of being an adult.

"Jo, are you feeling all right?" Meg asked as she, Jo, Beth, and Amy walked home from school.

"You don't want to be sick on your birthday," Beth said.

"That's right," Amy said. "Because if you're sick, then Hannah won't bake a cake and we won't get to eat any of it."

"I'm not sick," Jo said. "I just had a lot of thinking to do."

"I've never seen you think at lunch," Meg said. "Lunch is when you run around and play."

"I'm too old to do that anymore," Jo said. "Or I will be tomorrow, and since there's no school, I decided I should start being too old today."

"Then you're serious about being a lady," Meg said.

"Of course I am. I've learned my lesson. In fact, I've learned lessons no one has ever known before. I know why I've always been treated as a child."

"Because you are a child?" Beth asked.

Jo was a little annoyed that Beth could make such a casual remark about something Jo had agonized over. "It's more than that," she said. "It's because I've surrounded myself with childish things."

"Do you mean us?" Amy asked.

"You can't help being childish," replied Jo. "And no one expects you to be any different. No, I mean the time has come for me to give up all my childish things. As well as my childish ways. No one will ever treat me as an adult if they see me playing with dolls and toys and other foolish things."

"You're giving your toys away?" Amy asked. "May I have them?"

"Amy," Meg said. "It isn't nice to beg. Besides, Jo's things wouldn't interest you."

"I didn't even know you had any dolls," Beth said. "Not that I'm asking for them."

"I have a few things from my childhood," Jo said, marveling at how grown-up she sounded. "As soon as I get home I'm going to put them all in a box and tell Marmee to distribute them to the poor. That way I won't be tempted by seeing my sisters playing with them."

"That's very kind of you, Jo," Beth said.

"Very," said Meg, but Jo could tell from her tone she didn't understand what a grand gesture Jo was making. That was fine. Joan of Arc probably hadn't received much understanding from her big sister either.

CHAPTER 5

"*M*armee, Marmee!" Jo shouted as she reached the house.

"Remember, Jo, ladies don't shout," Meg scolded.

Jo stamped her foot in anger.

"And they don't stamp, either," Meg said.

"Don't worry, Jo," Beth said. "We know it can't be easy becoming a lady in just one day."

"Well, I intend to," Jo said. "Marmee," she said in a far quieter, more ladylike voice.

"Yes, Jo?" Marmee said, joining her daughters in the front hallway.

"Marmee, I've realized what I must do to be

an adult," Jo said. "I'm going to give away all my toys to the poor."

"That's a lovely idea," Marmee said. "But perhaps you should think about your decision just a little before you do it."

"There's nothing to think about," Jo replied. "I'm going to my room right now to pack everything away."

"I'll help," Amy said.

"I will also," Beth said.

"And I'll watch," Meg said.

Jo knew there would be no talking her sisters out of it, so she let them follow her to her room. "Amy, get a potato sack for me to put everything in," she said.

"I'm not leaving," Amy announced. "I want to be sure you don't give away any of my things by mistake."

"There's no reason for me to have any of your things," Jo said. "But I'll get the sack myself then." She ran out of the room and down the stairs, until she remembered she wasn't supposed to run anymore. So she walked slowly, not understanding how anyone managed to get anywhere without running.

Hannah supplied her with the sack, and Jo made every effort to walk as slowly back to her bedroom.

"My toys are in my trunk," Jo said as she entered and found her sisters sitting on the beds, waiting for her to begin. The trunk was kept at the foot of her bed. Each of her sisters had an identical one, and each kept her treasures in it.

Jo opened the trunk. Her sisters peered down from the beds to see what wonders it held.

"All it has are papers," Amy complained.

"Those are my plays and stories," Jo said. "The toys are underneath." She removed the papers, finding layer upon layer of them.

"You're not going to throw away your writing, are you, Jo?" Beth asked.

"No, of course not. Why should I?"

"Because you're always saying you're a better writer than you used to be," Beth said. "I was afraid you'd think your writing was childish."

"I'll keep it anyway," Jo said. "Here, I've gotten to my toys. See this wooden cow? It's definitely a toy, and I don't want or need it anymore."

"You never needed it," Meg said. "That was my cow. You took it from me years ago and never gave it back."

"You don't want it now, do you?" Jo asked.

Meg took the cow from Jo. "Yes, I do," she said. "It's my cow, and I'd like to keep it."

"Maybe you've been taking my things as well," Amy said.

"I have not," Jo said. "I don't even remember taking that silly cow."

"Jo's never taken any of my dolls," Beth said. "I remember every doll I've ever had, and I've never lost any of them."

"I'm sure I didn't take Meg's cow, either," Jo said. "She probably put it in my trunk by mistake, or gave me the cow when she grew too old for it."

"I'll never be too old for this cow," Meg

said. "I'll play with it with my own children someday."

"What else do you have?" Amy asked. "All I see are more papers."

"No, here's something," Jo said, although she was starting to feel discouraged by the lack of childish toys. "Wait, I'm digging it out." She pulled on a much-worn rag doll.

"That's Hortense!" Meg cried with delight.

"Don't tell me that's another of your toys," Amy said. "What a thief Jo is."

"Hortense is mine," Jo said. "Look at her, Meg. I haven't thought about her in years."

"Marmee made Hortense for Jo years and years ago," Meg said. "Jo was hardly more than a baby. She used to sleep with Hortense on her pillow and took her wherever she went."

"What an ugly doll," Amy said. "It looks as though you used to chew on it, Jo."

"She did," Meg said. "And she'd toss her about and kick her, and play roughly with her all the time. But every night, Hortense got the place of honor on Jo's pillow."

"I suppose I should give her away," Jo said, staring at the doll that had provided her with incredible fun and companionship. She remembered that she used to tell Hortense all her secrets. No matter how badly Jo had behaved, Hortense never seemed to mind.

"Nobody would want her," Amy said. "You might as well just throw her out."

"I'm afraid Amy's right," Meg said. "Not even Beth could fix that doll."

"Then I'll throw her away," Jo said, feeling a real lurch of sorrow as she tossed the doll into the potato sack.

"What about your other toys?" Amy asked. "I thought they were to go in the sack too."

"I don't seem to have any other toys," Jo said. "The rest of the trunk is full of papers."

"I'll take the sack back down," Beth said. "You see, Jo. You've been an adult all along. You just didn't know it."

"I still don't know it," Meg said, but Jo ignored her. If she didn't have childish things, surely that meant she wasn't a child after all.

CHAPTER 6

"*H*appy birthday, Jo, dearest," Marmee whispered into Jo's ear as she woke up the next morning.

"Happy birthday, Jo!" Meg cried.

Soon Beth, Amy, and Father had joined Marmee and Meg in wishing Jo the happiest of birthdays.

Jo sat up in bed and smiled. She was ten years old, at long last a grown-up. As soon as the thought crossed her mind, she stopped smiling.

"It's a beautiful day," Meg said. "Hurry, Jo. Get dressed, and we can play outside until lunch."

Jo did as she was instructed. The sun was shining, and a warm breeze made the clouds dance across the sky. It was a perfect day for rolling hoops or climbing trees or doing a thousand other things Jo had vowed no longer to do.

"I'll just sit and watch," she told her sisters as they took full advantage of the weather to exercise.

"Jo, it's all right to run and play," Meg said. "Just as long as you're careful with your clothing."

"No," Jo said. "You do what you want, but I'll sit still."

Meg shook her head. She found the hoops and sticks the girls needed to play, and soon they were having a fine time.

Jo knew she could join them, but she also knew if she did, she'd drop a hoop and start chasing after it, and one thing would lead to another, and she'd end up covered with grime. It was safer just to sit. Safer, and far more boring.

The morning passed slowly, but eventually

it was time for lunch. The girls all ate lightly, knowing that in honor of Jo's birthday, they'd be having a large supper, complete with birthday cake.

After lunch, Meg left to visit her friend Mary Howe. Beth busied herself tending to her dolls. Amy followed her because she enjoyed dressing and undressing the dolls in what she liked to think of as the latest French fashions.

Jo found a book and tried to content herself with reading under a tree. If she'd played all morning, she would have been ready for a quiet time. Instead she felt restless and longed for anything, even a cat chasing a rabbit, to take her mind off the long, long grown-up years that lay ahead of her.

"Jo!" Father called. "Are you doing anything?"

"Not a thing," Jo said.

"Then join me in the garden," Father said. "There's planting to be done."

Ordinarily Jo would have rushed to his

side. But this time she took a moment and said, "Let me put a smock on first, so I won't get my dress dirty."

"Very wise of you," Father answered. "I'll wait until you're ready."

Jo got a smock from the kitchen, slipped it over her dress, and met Father in the garden. He handed her a trowel, and they discussed the proper placing of the seeds to harvest the most vegetables in the coming summer.

It felt good to be in the garden with Father, digging in the dirt, feeling the sun warm the back of her neck. And Jo knew gardening was an adult activity. She wasn't sure it was something ladies did, but if it was good enough for her father, it was good enough for her.

"You are growing up," Father said as he and Jo stood up and stretched. "I do believe you've grown three inches since the last time we gardened together."

"There's more to growing than just getting taller," Jo said.

"That there is," Father replied. "And you're

growing in those ways as well. Thinking to put on a smock. Offering to give away your toys to children who don't have any."

"I didn't have any toys," Jo said. "Just a cow that belonged to Meg, and my doll Hortense." She felt the same lurch of sorrow at the mention of Hortense as she had the day before when she'd tossed the doll into the sack.

"That's because growing up isn't something that happens overnight," Father said. "Those three inches you've added to your height didn't happen in a moment. Growing up is full of stops and starts."

"The past two days have been all starts," Jo said. "When do you think I might have some stops?"

Father laughed. "I think you're due for some right now," he said. "Why don't you play with Beth and Amy? I'm sure they're ready for some running around by now, and there's still plenty of time left before your birthday supper."

"But what if I get dirty?" Jo asked.

"Don't take off the smock," Father suggested. "And don't chase any rabbits into the cellar."

"Thank you, Father!" Jo cried.

"Don't thank me," he said. "It's such a beautiful day, I think I'll join you in your games."

"Christopher Columbus!" Jo shouted with pleasure. She ran to the house and climbed the stairs two at a time. "Come, Beth, Amy," she said. "Father says we should be playing outside. He's going to join us in our games."

"Does this mean you're not an adult anymore?" Amy asked.

"Not for a while," Jo said. "I'm just going to be more careful until I'm older and taller."

"Oh, I'm so glad," Beth said. "You seemed terribly unhappy being an adult."

"It's very hard," Jo admitted. "And not a lot of fun."

"I have something for you," Beth said. She opened her trunk and pulled out an old and well-worn rag doll.

"Hortense!" Jo cried. "Oh, Bethy. I thought you threw her out."

"I couldn't," Beth said. "I was sure someday you'd want her again, since you loved her so much."

"Not as much as I love you," Jo replied. "Amy, Bethy, wait until you're ten. It's the best age ever!"

Beth's Birthday Wish

CHAPTER 1

"Sit down, sit down," Aunt March harrumphed as Beth and Amy inched their way into her back parlor. "To what do I owe the honor of this visit?"

"There's no reason," Amy said. "We just thought we'd pay a call."

Beth would have smiled if Aunt March hadn't terrified her so. The reason they had come was that their mother had insisted.

"You haven't called on Aunt March in weeks," Marmee had said. "You in particular, Beth. Aunt March wonders why she never sees you."

Beth didn't know why Aunt March ever

thought of her at all. Beth never had a word to say in Aunt March's presence. The thought of paying a call all by herself was so awful that Beth nearly wept with gratitude when Amy offered to come along. Amy actually seemed to enjoy Aunt March, and Beth knew Aunt March favored Amy as well.

"I'm pleased you actually remembered your old aunt," Aunt March said. "Sometimes I think I must be very unimportant to you all."

"Oh, no, Aunt March," Amy said. "It's just that between schoolwork, and tasks at home, and helping the less fortunate, we don't have much time for visits. Beth especially. She does quite a lot to help the poor. Don't you, Beth?"

Beth nodded. "That is to say, I mean, I do . . . ," she mumbled, after realizing how vain she must sound to claim she did anything as important as helping those who truly needed it.

Aunt March cackled. "Helping the less fortunate, indeed," she said. "Playing games is more like it. Running around like wild animals." But she smiled at Amy, so Beth assumed it was all right to be playing games and running around.

"Tell me, Beth," said Aunt March. "When you're not helping the less fortunate, what do you do that keeps you from paying calls on me?"

"I . . . I . . . ," Beth stammered.

"Beth's been terribly busy getting ready for her birthday," Amy put in. "Do you know, Aunt March, Beth will be ten tomorrow. How I wish I were ten already."

"You'll be ten soon enough," Aunt March replied. "Then twenty and thirty and an old lady before you know it. Well, Beth, have you great plans for your birthday?"

Beth shook her head.

"Perhaps you would like me to host a party for you," Aunt March said.

"Oh, no!" Beth cried. "That is to say, I mean, I just, I mean, you simply shouldn't. What I mean is that's very kind of you, but I simply . . ."

"You simply what?" Aunt March said. "Out with it, girl."

"I simply don't want any sort of party," Beth blurted out. "I don't like birthdays, especially my own, and I don't want anyone to make any sort of fuss. So thank you, Aunt March, but there's no need, and I'd be much happier if you completely forgot my birthday."

There was a stunned silence.

Beth couldn't remember ever having said so much to Aunt March before. And by the looks on their faces, neither could Aunt March or Amy.

"What do you mean you don't want a fuss?" asked Amy. "It's your birthday."

"I don't like fusses," Beth said, and as the words came out, she knew they were true. "I know I must have birthdays, because everyone gets older and that's just the way it is. But everyone doesn't have to celebrate, and I'm choosing not to."

"Why, Beth, I never knew you to have such firm opinions about anything," said Aunt March.

Beth was startled herself. But the more she

thought about it, the more she realized she meant every word she said.

"I hope everyone forgets it's my birthday," she said firmly. "I hope everyone treats it as an ordinary day."

"But, Beth," said Amy. "What about a cake? What about presents?"

"You may have them on your birthday," said Beth. "I want nothing on mine."

"I have no problem with Beth's decision," Aunt March said. "I gave up celebrating my birthday when my dear husband passed away. Beth, I assure you, I shall forget your impending birthday, and not even offer you the slightest token of celebration."

"Thank you," Beth said. Aunt March cackled some more, so Beth assumed there must be something funny in offering thanks for being ignored. Still, being ignored by Aunt March was no small blessing.

Amy didn't seem nearly as satisfied. "I know you'll change your mind," she said to Beth. "You'll want a cake and presents, Beth. You'll want a birthday celebration."

"No," Beth said. "I'm going to be ten. That's quite old enough to know what I want and don't want. And I don't want a fuss or presents or even a cake."

"But, Beth!" Amy cried.

"Amy, if those are your sister's wishes, you should respect them," said Aunt March. "You are, however, in luck in paying your call today. I have some lovely cakes in the house, every bit as fine as anything your Hannah can bake. We'll have them with tea, and they'll take your mind off that missing birthday cake."

"But it's not just the cake," Amy said.

"Then you must learn to respect your sister's wish," Aunt March replied. "Beth, I do trust you'll eat my cakes, if I assure you they have nothing to do with your birthday."

"Of course, Aunt March," Beth said. "And I'm sure I'll enjoy them very much indeed."

CHAPTER 2

"You'll change your mind," Amy said to Beth as they walked home from Aunt March's. "You'll wake up tomorrow morning and decide you want a fuss, and a cake. Hannah isn't baking until tomorrow anyway."

"I wish you'd listen to me," Beth said. "I've decided I don't want anybody to do anything about my birthday. Even Aunt March understood that. Why can't you?"

"Because I don't believe you," Amy said. "Everyone likes birthday festivities. Everyone likes cake and presents. You liked the cakes at Aunt March's."

"They were a special treat," Beth said. "And I do like cakes. But I don't like birthdays. At least not my own."

Amy shook her head. "You'll change your mind," she said. "I know you will."

"I will not!" Beth cried. "Just because you like birthdays doesn't mean I have to."

Amy stood absolutely still. "You don't have to shout."

"I'm sorry," Beth said. "I truly am."

"I forgive you." Amy smiled. "Besides, I know you're going to change your mind!"

"Amy!" And this time Beth really did shout. But Amy ignored her and ran the rest of the way home.

"How did your visit go?" Marmee asked as the girls entered their much humbler parlor.

"It was all right," Beth said. "Aunt March fed us cakes."

"Marmee, Beth says she doesn't want any sort of fuss for her birthday," Amy said. "She even told Aunt March that."

"What's this about a fuss?" Jo asked as she

and Meg walked in. "Did Aunt March make one of her fusses?"

"No, it was Beth," Amy said. "She made a fuss about not making a fuss."

"All I said was I didn't want any sort of birthday celebration," Beth said.

"No celebration?" Jo asked.

"But surely you'll want cake and presents," Meg said. "Believe me, Beth, I remember my wish to spend my tenth birthday without you, Jo, and Amy, and I was perfectly miserable."

"It's not that I don't want you around," Beth said. "I just want my birthday to be treated as any other day. Marmee, you always say we can have one special birthday wish. Well, mine is for my birthday to be no different than any other day."

"Tell her, Marmee, that we have to have a celebration," Amy demanded.

"If this is Beth's wish, we have to respect it," Marmee said slowly. "But I hope, Beth, that you'll think it over."

"I hope so too," said Jo. "Celebrations are

fun. And cakes are a rarity in this house. I'd hate to lose my chance to have one."

Beth felt the cake was a trap. If she agreed to one, there were sure to be games, and gifts, and Aunt March, and all kinds of things she preferred not to deal with.

"No cake," she said. "No party. No presents. Just an ordinary sort of day. That's my birthday wish, and Marmee says I can have what I want."

"But, Beth," Meg said.

"What?" Beth asked. "Do you want cake also? Then pay a call on Aunt March. She has cake enough for all of you."

"It's not that," Meg said. "It's just that birthdays are important. And joyous. And I don't see why you don't want any fun on yours."

Beth wasn't sure why either, but she knew this birthday was becoming less and less fun. "Please," she said. "Please respect my wish. Do I ask that much of you?"

"You never ask anything of us," Jo responded. "You're an angel, Bethy. If you want an invisible birthday, that is what you'll have."

"But, Jo," Amy said.

"Hush." Jo frowned. "Beth is turning ten. She's old enough to know what she wants."

"Thank you, Jo," Beth said. "I knew you'd understand."

CHAPTER 3

"So, Beth," said Father that evening at supper. "Tomorrow is the big day. You'll be ten at long last. Have you given any thought to how you want us to celebrate?"

Jo burst out laughing. "Bethy's done nothing but think about it," she said.

"What's this?" Father asked. "Do you have elaborate plans, Beth? Are we to have a truly splendid party in your honor?"

Now even Amy laughed.

"I want nothing, Father," Beth replied. "No party, no celebration."

"Beth made that very clear to us this afternoon," Marmee said. "But you were out, and I haven't had the opportunity to discuss it with you."

"I'm sorry to hear you feel that way, Beth," said Father. "I like birthdays. I like celebrations."

"I'm sorry, Father," Beth said. "If you really feel I should have a party, of course I will, to make you happy."

"Yes, Father," Amy said. "It would make all of us happy if Beth only agrees."

"Now, Amy," said Father. "I can hardly order one of my little women to have a party she has no desire for. I'm afraid we shall all have to live with the disappointment."

Beth hated disappointing her father. He asked so little of her. "I suppose we could have a cake," she said. "If Hannah doesn't mind baking it."

"Hannah won't mind," Meg said. "I'm sure of it. After all, she's been planning to bake one tomorrow for weeks now."

"No," Father said. "We can't have a cake just to satisfy my desires. That wouldn't be fair to Beth."

"Marmee," Amy said. "Please tell Beth she simply has to change her mind."

"Oh, Amy," Marmee said. "You can't force someone to have a good time."

"I will have a good time," Beth said. "Just a quiet one. Why doesn't anyone understand that?"

"Because we all like fusses," said Jo.

There was a knock on the door. "I'll get it," Meg said. When she returned to the dining room, she was accompanied by Mr. Marshall.

Mr. Marshall owned a bookstore in town. He had a rule forbidding anyone under the age of ten to enter his shop, which was fine with Beth, since he scared her. But she knew that her father was fond of him, and Mr. Marshall and Jo were friends as well.

"I'm sorry to interrupt your supper," Mr. Marshall said, joining the family at the table.

"Nonsense," Father said. "There's plenty for you."

Mr. Marshall smiled. "Thank you. I really didn't mean to stay. I simply wanted to bring you the book you ordered. You said you wanted it by tomorrow, and I wasn't sure you'd have time to stop by the shop."

"What book?" Father asked.

"The book of hymns," Mr. Marshall replied. "A present, I think you said."

"Oh, yes, that. You know, I'd almost forgotten about it."

"The book was published in New York," Mr. Marshall explained, "and some of my New York orders take forever to arrive. But this one is here on time. I hope the person you honor with it will enjoy it. It looks like a fine collection."

"Who is it for, Father?" Jo asked. Her eyes then widened. "Oh, dear."

"Oh, dear, what?" Amy asked. "Oh, you mean . . . ? Oh!"

"Quite a lot of 'oh's around here," said Mr. Marshall. "Have I caused a problem by bringing the book directly to you, Mr. March?"

"Not at all," Father replied.

"A book of hymns is such a lovely present," Meg said. "If it's given to the right person, that is."

"Of course the right person has to *want* a present," said Jo, and burst into laughter.

"Now, girls," Marmee said. "Thank you, Mr. Marshall, for bringing us the book. And please forgive all our mysterious comments. I'm afraid you walked into the middle of a family discussion about presents."

"I love presents myself," said Mr. Marshall. "They usually accompany a big to-do. Of course right now, I like it best when people come to my shop to purchase presents for others. As Mr. March was kind enough to do."

"Father, the book is for me?" Beth asked.

"It is," Father said. "Who else is more deserving of a new book of hymns?"

"I know you told us you didn't want any presents," Marmee said. "But perhaps, Bethy, dearest, you could think of this as a present you'd be giving all of us. You're the one who'll be playing the hymns on the piano for years to come. And we'll be the ones enjoying your playing."

"Do accept the gift," Meg said. "You know how much I love singing when you play, Beth. It would be a kindness to me if you had a new book of hymns to play from."

"I'd appreciate it also," Mr. Marshall said. "If you don't accept it—and I must admit, I don't know why anyone would turn down such a fine gift—I would feel obliged to take the book back. It's an excellent collection of hymns, and I'm sure it will find a home, but frankly, I had counted on the money from the sale today."

Beth stared at Mr. Marshall. It sounded as though his very livelihood depended on her accepting a birthday present. "All right," she said. "But this is the only gift I want. Marmee, please tell me you don't have any gifts for me."

"I can't tell you that," Marmee said. "But whatever else you may be receiving can wait until you're more in the mood for presents."

"Christmas, perhaps," Jo said, and began laughing again.

Mr. Marshall shook his head. "Mr. March," he said. "You have four fine daughters. But no one would ever mistake you for an average American family."

"We wouldn't have it any other way," Father said, and his laugh was one of pure pleasure.

CHAPTER 4

*B*eth woke up the next morning with a start. She knew it was a special day, but for a moment she couldn't remember why. Then it came back to her. It was her birthday. She was ten.

She looked out the window. The sun was up. Birds were singing. And inside the house she heard the sounds of her family rising, preparing for their day. Amy was still asleep, so Beth decided to slip out of bed and escape from their bedroom while she had the chance.

But quiet though Beth tried to be, Amy heard her anyway. "Beth," she said. "Have you changed your mind?"

"No," Beth said, a little more sharply than she intended.

"Then I can't wish you a happy birthday?" Amy asked.

Beth looked over at her little sister. "Do you still want to?" she asked.

Amy nodded.

"All right, then," Beth said. "But that's all you can say about it."

"Happy birthday, Beth," Amy said.

"Thank you," Beth replied.

There was a knock on the door, but before Beth or Amy had a chance to say a word, Meg and Jo burst in. "Happy birthday, Bethy," Jo said without waiting for permission.

"Yes, happy birthday," Meg said. "It's so hard to believe our Beth is ten already."

"She hasn't changed her mind," Amy said mournfully.

"Then I shan't say another word," Jo declared. "Except to remind both of you that birthday or no, we all have to go to school."

Beth usually dreaded school, but today it seemed like a fine idea. "I'll be ready before

Amy," she said, dashing to her wardrobe for a dress.

School was a relief after all the fuss that had been made over not making a fuss. Beth had few friends in school, and no one seemed to know or care what day it was in her life. Her teacher, knowing how shy she was, never called on her, and Beth contented herself by paying attention to her schoolwork.

At lunch she did regret the decision not to allow Hannah to bake a cake. But she reminded herself of the cakes she'd had at Aunt March's. Surely no one should have two cakes in two days, even if one of those days was her birthday. And when she thought about the book of hymns that awaited her, she wished, just for a moment, that she hadn't refused all other presents. But then she felt greedy for wanting anything more, and was glad the lovely book of hymns was a present she could share with her whole family.

Birthdays certainly were difficult. Beth was glad they happened only once a year.

As the sisters walked home from school,

Amy raced alongside Beth. "Have you changed your mind yet?" she asked.

"Amy!" Beth said.

"Forgive Amy," Meg said. "You know how she loves birthdays."

"Birthdays are the most fun of anything," Amy declared. "I think it's mean of you, Beth, not to have one."

"That's Beth, all right," said Jo. "She's so mean."

"Oh, Jo, do you really think so?" Beth asked.

"No, of course not," Jo replied. "And neither does Amy. Do you, Amy?"

"I think you're all mean!" Amy cried, and she ran off.

"Jo," Meg said. "Perhaps you should catch up with her."

"No, let her be," Jo replied. "It's Beth's day, and we should respect her wishes. Amy needs to learn she can't always have things her way."

"It isn't just Amy," said Meg.

"Please," Beth said. "Don't talk about me as though I weren't here."

"That's what happens with invisible birthdays," Jo said. "The birthday person becomes invisible as well."

"I wish birthdays had never been invented," Meg said. "I remember when I turned ten. Nothing went the way I wanted it."

"I just wanted to be an adult," said Jo. "And when I tried to behave like one, I was miserable. You're right, Meg. Birthdays are far too complicated."

"They'd be simple if we just ignored them," Beth said. "Which is all I ever wanted."

"Consider it ignored," Jo said.

"Just the way you want it," said Meg. "And we hope that makes you happy, Beth."

"It does," Beth replied. But she didn't feel happy at all.

C H A P T E R   5

*B*eth went up to her room as soon as she got home, hoping for some peace and quiet. But she found Amy lying on her bed.

"I'm sorry," Beth said, not quite sure what she was apologizing about.

"No, you're not!" Amy said, and to Beth's surprise and horror, Amy began to cry.

"What is it?" Beth asked. "Why are you so upset?"

"Because you haven't changed your mind!" Amy sobbed. "You are mean and selfish, no matter what you think."

"I'm sorry," Beth said again, and backed out

111

of the bedroom. She couldn't bear to see Amy cry, and she hated the thought that she was responsible.

Downstairs, she found Meg and Jo sitting in the parlor. "Amy's crying," she announced. "Why is my birthday so important to her?"

Meg and Jo exchanged looks. "We were hoping we wouldn't have to tell you," Meg said.

"Amy came up with a special gift for your birthday," Jo said. "She's been excited about it for weeks now."

"I didn't know."

"It's not your fault," Jo said. "Amy was determined to keep it a surprise. And for once she managed."

"I'm sure if you'd known, none of this would have happened," Meg said.

"No, of course not," Jo said. "You never would have done anything to disappoint Amy."

"Or us, either," Meg said. "I do have to admit, Beth, I am disappointed."

"We all are," Jo said. "And not just because we won't be getting any birthday cake."

"I don't know what to do anymore," Beth said. "I didn't want to upset any of you."

"Maybe you should talk things over with Marmee," Meg said. "But she's out."

"Father's in his study," Jo said. "I talked to him on my tenth birthday, and he was a great help. Maybe he can help you, Bethy."

"That's a good idea." Beth left her sisters and knocked on Father's study door.

"Come in."

"Father, may I speak to you?" Beth asked, opening the door.

"Of course, child. Sit down. Tell me what's the matter. You look downcast, not at all the way a person should look on her birthday."

"It's my birthday that's made me downcast," Beth said. "Father, was it wrong of me to want no fuss? Amy is crying, and Meg and Jo are upset also, and I know it's my fault, but I don't understand why."

"Oh, Beth," said Father. "Is it really that

113

important to you that no one make a fuss over your birthday?"

"I thought it was," Beth said.

"Do you know why?" Father asked. "I don't remember your saying anything about it before yesterday."

"I hadn't given it a thought," Beth said. "Then Amy brought it up at Aunt March's, and I never like going over there. Aunt March scares me so. I know I should love her, because she's my great-aunt, but I never know what to say when I'm with her."

"Aunt March has that effect on people," Father said. "She means no harm, but she can be somewhat frightening."

"But none of this is her fault," said Beth. "I know that. It was my idea to have no fuss made. Father, you've taught us to be modest and not to be greedy. But birthdays are all about being the center of attention. I love your present, Father. But I don't want everyone to feel they have to give me something."

"Do you like offering people presents for their birthdays?" Father asked.

Beth nodded.

"Do you know why?" Father asked. "Sometimes we do things simply because we're supposed to, and we don't give any thought as to why we do them."

"I only give presents to people I love," Beth said. "I guess I want them to know how much I love them."

Father nodded. "That's why I like birthdays," he said. "Because it's a day when we can declare our love for someone special. Today it's your birthday, and it's the day we all want to show our love for you."

"So am I being selfish for not wanting anything?"

"It isn't enough just to love," Father said. "Sometimes we have to be loved as well."

Beth sighed. "Life certainly is complicated," she said.

"That it is," Father said. "And love makes it better, but not any simpler."

"Father," Beth said as she rose.

"Yes?"

"Aren't you going to wish me a happy birthday?"

Father smiled a huge smile and got up from behind his desk. He gave Beth a big hug. "Have a very, very happy birthday, my darling daughter!"

"Well," Jo said as Beth walked back into the parlor. "Did talking to Father help?"

Beth grinned. "Is that any way to talk to me on my birthday?" she asked. "Aren't you going to wish me a happy day again?"

"The happiest!" Jo said.

"Happy birthday, Beth!" Meg said.

"My, my," Marmee said, entering the house. "Everyone seems so cheerful."

"And why shouldn't we be cheerful?" Jo asked. "It's our Bethy's birthday, after all."

"And we intend to celebrate," Meg added.

"I don't suppose Hannah could still make a special supper?"

"Did I hear you calling me?" Hannah asked from the kitchen.

"We were just wondering about supper," Jo called back.

Hannah entered the parlor. "I hope chicken will do," she said. "And roasted potatoes. Carrots, fresh bread, and a big birthday cake, of course."

"But, Hannah!" Beth said. "I thought you were told not to make a fuss."

"No one told me any such thing," Hannah answered. "And even if they had, I'd have paid no mind. Birthdays are made for cakes, and cakes for birthdays, and there won't be one without the other as long as I'm in this kitchen!"

"Hooray for Hannah!" Jo cried.

"I'd better tell Amy," Beth said. "She'll want to know what a wonderful celebration I'm going to have."

"And I'm going to find your presents," Marmee said. "I'm glad we can give them to you on this special day."

118

"I'd love it if you did." Beth smiled at them all and went upstairs to get Amy.

"Amy, please come downstairs," Beth said as she entered their bedroom. Amy was lying on her bed, her face to the wall. "Marmee's going to give me my birthday presents, and Hannah has made the most wonderful supper, and we're going to have birthday cake after all."

Amy lifted her head and wiped at her tear-stained face. "Oh, Amy," Beth said, going over to her sister. "I'm sorry. I should have realized how important this was to you."

"Jo always says I'm so selfish," Amy cried. "And this once I came up with an idea for your present, and it was my idea, not Jo's, or Meg's, or Marmee's. It was mine, and Meg and Jo agreed it was wonderful. I was so proud, and then you said you didn't want anything."

"You know something?" Beth said. "I was wrong. I do want presents. And I especially want yours because you're so clever. So if it isn't too late, could I have whatever it is?"

Amy nodded. "It's downstairs," she said. "Marmee has it."

"Well then, let's join everyone," Beth said. "Supper is just about ready anyway."

The sisters raced down into the parlor. "Marmee, Marmee!" Amy cried. "Where's Beth's present?"

"It's right here," Marmee said. She stood by Father's side, both of them smiling.

Amy grabbed a big box from Marmee's arms. It had a beautiful bow on it. "This is from all of us," Amy declared as she handed the box to Beth. "Meg and Jo and me. But it was my idea. Wasn't it, Meg?"

"It certainly was," Meg said.

"And a fine idea it is," Jo said. "Open it, Bethy."

Beth carefully untied the ribbon and opened the box.

"Oh, my," she said as she carefully lifted the most beautiful doll she'd ever seen from its wrapping. "I've never seen one so lovely."

"We chose her together," Amy said. "Do you love her, Beth?"

"How could I not?" Beth said. Her eyes filled with tears. "She's perfect."

"She has a name, too," Jo said. "Amy named her."

"Mamie Jo," Amy said. "That's Meg and Amy and Jo put together."

"Mamie Jo," Beth said. "Oh, Marmee, look at her. Her dress is silk. And it has real lace on it."

"We took all the money we had saved up," Amy said. "Oh, Beth, you look just the way I wanted you to look when we gave Mamie Jo to you."

"Then you must have wanted me to look happy," Beth said. "Because that's exactly how I feel. I really love birthdays."

Amy's smile lit the room. "I knew it!" she crowed. "I knew sooner or later you'd change your mind!"

And Beth was truly glad she had.

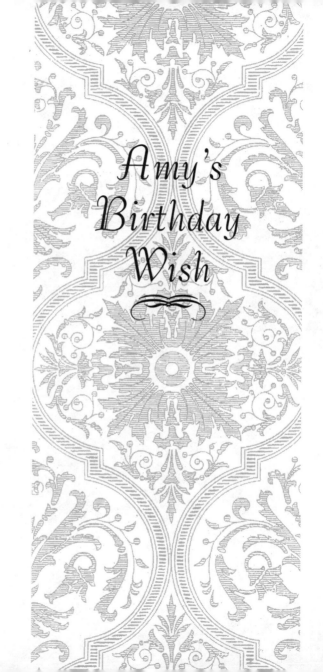

Amy's
Birthday
Wish

CHAPTER 1

It wasn't easy, but Amy held off until April first before making her announcement. "There're less than two weeks to my birthday!" she cried.

"Yes, Amy, we know," Jo replied with a roll of her eyes.

"Thirteen days," Amy continued. "In thirteen days, I'll be ten years old."

"That's April fourteenth," Jo said in a stage whisper to Meg and Beth. "Thirteen days from now."

"I just wanted to give you some warning," Amy said. "Think how terrible it would be if you forgot and my birthday just crept up on you."

"That isn't very likely," Meg replied. "Since every year, on April first, you remind us your birthday is only thirteen days away."

"That's not true," Jo said. "There was at least one year when Amy made her announcement fourteen days ahead. I remember because it was so unusual."

"Stop teasing Amy," said Beth. "I'm excited for her that her birthday is coming so soon. It's an important time, turning ten."

"Don't remind me," said Jo. "I still shudder when I think of the horrible mess I made of my tenth birthday."

"Mine wasn't the success I wanted it to be," Meg said.

"And mine was the worst of all," said Beth with a laugh. "I actually made Amy cry."

"I've learned from all of you," said Amy. "And I intend to have a perfectly splendid tenth birthday. Oh, Marmee, do come in. We're talking about my birthday. It's only thirteen days away."

Marmee smiled as she entered the parlor. "I'm aware of that, dearest," she said. "You didn't have to leave that note on my pillow this morning to remind me."

"Oh, Amy, you are shameless," declared Jo. "Of all people, Marmee would never forget your birthday."

"Marmee has many things on her mind," Amy pointed out. "Her birthday, and Father's, and Meg's, and yours, and Beth's, and Aunt March's, and Hannah's. And I knew she'd be positively heartbroken if she forgot mine. So I left a little note. That wasn't bad of me, was it, Marmee?"

"Not bad," Marmee replied. "But not necessary, either. I'd hardly forget my youngest's birthday."

Amy sighed. "No matter how old I get, I'll always be the youngest," she said. "But ten is a very mature age, and I really do think I should have a party this year."

Her sisters all broke out in laughter. "You've had a party every year since you've learned how to talk," Jo said. "You've never been satisfied with a simple family celebration."

"Oh, I'd like one of those also!" Amy said with a clap of her hands. "But my friends would be disappointed if there was no party. And my birthday falls on a Saturday this year. Isn't that wonderfully convenient? How many friends may I invite, Marmee? I do want this to be the best birthday party ever."

"Five friends," Marmee replied. "With you that will make six. And of course Meg, Jo, and Beth are invited as well, for a total of nine girls."

"Five friends," Amy said, clearly not interested in her sisters' attendance. "It will be so difficult to choose. Hearts will be broken, Marmee."

"That's all we can afford," Marmee replied. "And small parties are more fun, anyway. Big parties are noisy, and feelings are always hurt when someone is ignored or overlooked when choosing sides for a game."

"Besides, Amy, it isn't as though you were coming out," said Jo. "Maybe someday there'll be a big ball in your honor, but right now, you're only turning ten."

"You say that because already you're thirteen," complained Amy. "Soon you'll be attending balls. I have forever to go before I'm invited to a ball. This birthday party is my one chance to be social and have my friends by my side."

"And besides, the more friends, the more presents," Jo said.

Amy blushed. "Not all of us are as greedy as you are, Jo March," she said. "I want to share my happiness with my friends and sisters. Is that so wrong?"

"It's not wrong at all," said Marmee. "But you're going to have to share your happiness with no more than five friends."

"I could stay away from the party," Beth suggested. "Then Amy could have another friend come in my place."

"What a temptation!" Jo cried. "We could all stay away, hide in some cupboard somewhere, and Amy could fill the house with all her friends instead."

"No," said Marmee, in the kind of voice that Amy knew meant the discussion had ended. "Five friends, Saturday afternoon, games, presents, cake, and ice cream."

"Ice cream!" Amy said, and any disappointment she might have felt over having such a small party vanished instantly. "Oh, Marmee, could we really have ice cream?"

Marmee nodded. "A new store opened in town, selling ice cream and oysters," she said. "Aunt March told me their products are of the highest quality. I think for an event as special as a tenth birthday, we might manage some ice cream to go with our cake."

Amy gave her mother a hug. "Ice cream," she said. "Oh, Marmee, ice cream is so elegant. I know this will be the best birthday party ever."

"At least until you turn eleven," Jo said, but Amy no longer minded the teasing. Her birthday was thirteen days away, and she would have a party, with ice cream to go with her cake. Life could not be better.

CHAPTER 2

*A*my went to school the next day still debating which friends she should invite to her party. Katy Brown and Mary Kingsley were the girls she was closest to, and they had come to her birthday parties in years past. But that left three other girls to invite, and those were harder choices.

Amy looked at her classmates as her teacher droned on about states' rights and the recent election that had put Abraham Lincoln into the White House. Under ordinary circumstances, Amy might have been interested. Beth had had an encounter with Abraham Lincoln, and he'd visited their school while campaigning for the presidency. And for months discussions at the dinner table had focused on Mr. Lincoln and the risk of a war over slavery.

But current events paled in comparison to a birthday that was merely twelve days away, and a party complete with cake and ice cream. Katy and Mary, for certain. But who else to invite?

Amy glanced over and noticed Jenny Snow. Jenny was smart and pretty and came from a wealthy and respectable family. Amy had longed for Jenny's friendship, but Jenny had never been as impressed with Amy as Amy was with Jenny.

Amy thought fondly of her home. It was a dear place, comfortable, full of books, with walls covered in artwork (some of it by Amy herself). She had never been inside Jenny's home, but she had walked past it many times and knew it was three times the size of the Marches' and probably ten times as well furnished. And while the Marches made do with one servant, the Snows probably had six or more. What would Jenny think of the

Marches' house? Would she like Amy any more or less if she saw how they lived?

It was a difficult decision, and Amy wished she had more time to ponder her choices. She dearly wanted Jenny to be her friend. But Amy was not accustomed to feeling ashamed of the way her family lived. She knew there were far more important things than wealth and possessions. Still, she wasn't at all sure Jenny Snow knew that.

Amy watched as Jenny leaned over and whispered something to her best friend, Susie Perkins. Susie was as rich as Jenny, and the two girls did everything together. If Amy invited Jenny, she'd have to invite Susie as well. That would leave only one other girl to invite.

As Amy looked at every girl in her class, she pictured them on her lawn, in her parlor, playing games, bringing gifts, and eating cake and ice cream. It had to be just the right girl, someone with breeding, someone from a fine family, but not a snob. Jenny and Susie were snobs enough for one party.

Amy finally decided on Rebecca Winthrop. Marmee was close friends with Mrs. Winthrop, and Amy knew she'd be pleased by the choice. Rebecca's family didn't have a great deal of money, but even Aunt March approved of them. Amy suspected Marmee wouldn't particularly care for Jenny and Susie, but inviting Rebecca would make up for a lot.

Her decision having been made, Amy tried to concentrate on what her teacher was saying. She knew the issue of states' rights and slavery was important, but it had nothing really to do with her. Perhaps, eleven years hence, when Amy was twenty-one, women would be allowed to vote, and Amy would have a say in the way her country was governed. But she was only ten (in a mere twelve days), and not even Aunt March was permitted to vote, so it was hard for Amy to feel it really mattered.

Eventually it was lunchtime, and Amy was delighted to have a chance to get up and stretch. Most of the boys went outside to play, but the girls Amy needed to talk to remained in the classroom. Amy went to Katy and Mary first. They were the easiest girls to invite, and she wanted to be sure they'd accept before moving on to Jenny and Susie.

"I'm having a birthday party," she told them. "On April thirteenth, which is a Saturday and less than two weeks from now. I'll be ten, you know. Marmee said I could invite five girls to the party, and of course, you two were my first choices. We're going to have cake and ice cream. Please say you'll come."

"Of course I will," said Mary. "I come every year."

"I told my mama your birthday was in less than two weeks," Katy declared. "And Mama said you had your friends very well trained if we could remember that without any coaching from you."

Amy wasn't sure that was a compliment. "Does that mean you'll come also?" she asked.

Katy nodded. "I was sure you'd invite me,"

she said. "I already told Mama just what I want to give you."

"Who else are you inviting?" Mary asked. "It must be hard to pick just the right girls."

"I thought Jenny and Susie and Rebecca," Amy said.

"You had best ask them right away," Katy said. "Jenny always has a busy social calendar, and Susie won't go to a party unless Jenny is there."

"Rebecca is a nice girl," Mary said. "You can leave her for last."

"Go now," Katy urged Amy. "Jenny and Susie are laughing. That must mean they're in a good mood."

"Wish me luck," said Amy, and she crossed the classroom to where Jenny and Susie were eating.

"It's Amy March," Jenny said. "It must be April."

"Why do you say that?" Amy asked.

"Because every April you have a birthday party," Jenny said. "Not that we've ever been invited."

"It breaks our hearts every year," Susie added. "Hearing all those wonderful plans for your party and knowing we're not to share in the fun."

"I'm sorry for not having invited you in the past," Amy said. "But this year, I am. In fact, I came over to invite you. My party is on Saturday the thirteenth, and there'll be games and cake and ice cream. I hope you can make it."

"I suppose it's possible," Jenny said. "It will be the social event of the season."

"This year and next," said Susie.

"How fortunate we are to have finally been invited," said Jenny. "Who else has been asked?"

"Mary and Katy," Amy replied. "And I'm about to ask Rebecca as well."

"What fun!" said Susie with a clap of her hands. "Finally we've been asked to Amy March's famous birthday party."

"You should ask Rebecca now," said Jenny, pushing Amy toward her. "She's alone so you won't be hurting anyone else's feelings."

"As *our* feelings have been hurt throughout the years," said Susie. "Hurry, Amy."

So Amy walked over to Rebecca, who was indeed alone, reading a book and nibbling on a sandwich.

"Hello, Rebecca, my birthday is on Saturday, the thirteenth," Amy said. "I'm having a party and was hoping you could attend. Marmee has limited my guests to five, and I do want you to be one of them."

Rebecca smiled. "I'd like to come very much," she said. "Thank you, Amy, for thinking of me. Who else will be attending?"

"Mary and Katy and Jenny and Susie," Amy replied. "We'll play games and eat cake and ice cream."

"Let me know when to arrive, and I'll be sure to be there," said Rebecca. "Perhaps my mother can help yours with the arrangements."

"That's very kind of you," Amy said. She thanked Rebecca and walked back to Mary and Katy.

"They all accepted," she told them. "It's going to be an absolutely splendid birthday."

"I can hardly wait," said Katy, and Amy knew she meant it. But Amy also knew no one was more impatient for the great day than she was.

*A*my decided to pay a call on Aunt March after school that day. It was true she had visited her great-aunt a week before, but she knew Aunt March enjoyed her visits. Besides, Amy had not mentioned her birthday previously, and she was certain it would upset Aunt March fiercely if she failed to remember Amy's birthday.

Aunt March's butler ushered Amy into the back parlor, where Aunt March was busy doing her needlepoint. Of all the sisters, Amy actually enjoyed calling on Aunt March. She loved Aunt March's gracious home and the well-mannered servants, and she loved

Aunt March as well, sharp-tongued though she was.

"This is a pleasant surprise," said Aunt March after Amy had kissed her on her cheek. "You're coming round often these days."

"I hope you don't mind. I wouldn't want you to tire of my company."

"Not at all, child," said Aunt March. "Sit by me and tell me all that is new with you."

"Things couldn't be better," said Amy. "At long last, it's April. April is my favorite month. It's the first month of spring. The flowers start to bloom, and the trees to bud, and the birds to sing."

"And if I remember correctly, you have a birthday in April," Aunt March said, leaning forward.

Amy lowered her eyes. "How kind of you to remember," she said.

"As though you'd ever let me forget," said Aunt March. "You pay a call on me every year at this time, sing the praises of the month, and then remind me of your birthday. It's on the thirteenth, I believe."

"Yes, Aunt March," Amy said. "I'll be ten."

"Ten. A fine age. When I was ten, Thomas Jefferson was president. A good man from the state of Virginia. And now his fellow Virginians are seceding from this country and trying to form one of their own."

Politics again. Was there no escaping them? "Did you have a birthday party when you were ten?" Amy asked.

"I suppose," Aunt March replied. "Although I have no memories of it, and my parents didn't believe in idle celebrations. I suppose you'll be having a party. Are you here to invite me?"

"Would you like to attend?" Amy asked. "We'll be having cake and ice cream, and five of my best friends are coming."

"Ladies all, I trust," said Aunt March. "From the good families of Concord?"

Amy nodded. "All girls you would approve of," she said. "I'd truly be pleased if you joined us."

"You are a good girl," Aunt March declared. "However, you don't need a great-aunt to make your birthday party a success, so I'll decline your sweet invitation."

Amy hadn't really thought Aunt March would accept. But her presence would probably have impressed Jenny and Susie.

"Ten is quite a grown-up age," Aunt March said. "You're not a little girl anymore."

"I'm glad you realize that," Amy said. "At home, they treat me like a baby, simply because I'm the youngest."

"I was the youngest in my family," Aunt March said. "With three brothers and two sisters older than I, I longed for someone younger than myself. Now it seems I'm the oldest person I know!"

Amy couldn't imagine Aunt March ever having been young. Still, it made her smile to think of it.

"Tell me whom you've invited?" Aunt March asked. "Perhaps I'll recognize some of the names."

"I should think you'd recognize them all," replied Amy. "Katy Brown and Mary Kingsley and Jenny Snow and Susie Perkins and Rebecca Winthrop."

Aunt March pursed her lips. "All fine families," she finally said. "The Snows are new money, but Mrs. Snow's great-grandfather was a second cousin of my grandmother's, so they're respectable enough. I can see you've chosen your friends wisely."

"I'm pleased you approve."

Aunt March smiled. "I know you mean that," she said. "And it makes me happy to hear you say it. Suppose I loan your mother one of my fine lace tablecloths, and some of my china and silver for the occasion. Do you think your friends would notice and appreciate such treasures?"

"Oh, Aunt March, would you?" Amy cried. "They would all be so impressed. Your things are ever so lovely!"

"Not my best china, or silver, my dear," said Aunt March. "But better than you have, I'm sure, and nice enough to make a party that much more special."

"We'll take good care of everything," Amy promised. "And it will all be returned to you just the way you loaned it. Thank you, Aunt March. That's the loveliest present you could have given me."

"There might be another present or two on your birthday as well," Aunt March said. "I have a soft spot in my heart for you, my child."

"I love you, Aunt March," Amy said. "Oh, wait until I tell my friends. They'll be so excited, knowing we're using your lace and china and silver for my party."

"Someday you'll own such things," Aunt March said. "But in the meantime, the use of mine will have to do."

"It will do perfectly," said Amy. "Oh, Aunt March, this is going to be the best birthday ever!"

CHAPTER 4

*A*my woke up on the morning of her birthday and stared out the window at a cloudless blue sky. She could tell from the temperature in her bedroom that the sun was casting off heat as well as light. The day was perfect, everything she could have dreamed of for her tenth birthday.

Beth was still asleep, so Amy tiptoed out of the room and went downstairs. There was already a hubbub of activity. One of Aunt March's servants had arrived, carrying the linens, china, and silver that promised to make Amy's party so special. Father was helping the manservant unload, and Marmee was in the kitchen with Hannah, discussing preparations.

Amy took a quick look at the boxes that were being carried in and decided to check on things in the kitchen. Hannah already had the fire going, and the ingredients for the birthday cake had been set out.

"Do you have everything for the cake?" Amy asked, nervously checking the table where the supplies had been placed.

"If you mean flour and sugar and eggs, yes, I do," said Hannah.

"I know that," Amy said. "I meant the coin and the button and the ring and the thimble."

Hannah snorted. "I've never heard of such a foolish custom before," she said. "Putting silly things like that in one of my cakes."

"Oh, Marmee," Amy said. "Please tell Hannah she absolutely has to. It's the fashion in Germany. If you get a slice of cake with the coin, that means you'll be rich. The button means you'll be poor, and the ring means you'll get married, and the thimble means you won't. Marmee, I just have to have my cake that way."

"Happy birthday, my dear Amy," Marmee said instead. "Do I get a kiss from the birthday girl?"

"Of course," Amy said. "Isn't it just the most beautiful day, Marmee?"

"That it is," Marmee said. "Hannah, where did we put the coin and all the other trinkets for the cake?"

"They're here, freshly washed," said Hannah. "Although I still think it's a foolish idea. What if someone bites into the thimble and breaks a tooth?"

"Then they'll be sure to remain unmarried," said Amy. "Oh, Hannah, you are a dear to go to so much bother for my birthday. I know it's going to be the most delicious cake ever baked."

"And the most dangerous," Hannah muttered, but then she smiled at Amy. "Happy birthday to you," she said. "It's hard to believe our little Amy is already ten."

"Where should I put all this?" Father asked, carrying two boxes in his arms. "Is there room in the kitchen, or should I store them in the parlor?"

"There's space here for the time being," Marmee said. "Amy, you will remember to write Aunt March a note of thanks."

"Of course, Marmee."

"Happy birthday, Amy," Father said, giving her a hug. "Are you ready for your celebration?"

"I wish the party had already begun!" Amy cried. "Oh, Father, this is going to be my best birthday ever."

"It won't be for lack of preparation if it isn't," said Jo, entering the kitchen. "Happy birthday, Amy. I hope it's all you want it to be."

"It will be, I just know it," Amy said.

"Happy birthday," said Meg, and Beth repeated the wish as they crowded into the kitchen.

Amy had never felt happier. The day was off to a fine start and would only get better.

"Perhaps you should get dressed," Marmee suggested. "Unless you want to celebrate your birthday in your nightgown."

"Oh, Marmee!" Amy said. She left the kitchen and rushed up the stairs to her room. Meg, Jo, and Beth, Marmee and Father, all followed her. Amy thought this strange but assumed they simply had things to attend to.

So her surprise was great when she spotted a large box on her bed. Amy raced over to it, now aware why her sisters and parents were watching her so closely.

She opened the box and found a brand-new dress. It was blue gray and matched the color of her eyes. "Oh, Marmee!" she cried. "Oh, Marmee! I've never seen such a beautiful dress."

"We wanted you to have something special to wear today," Marmee said. "You have far too many hand-me-downs and not nearly enough new dresses."

"I'll cherish it forever," said Amy, holding the dress close to her body as she whirled around.

"If only you could wear it forever," said Jo. "For when you outgrow it, there'll be no one to hand it down to."

"We don't have to worry about that today," Marmee said. "Put the dress on, dear, and let us see if it fits."

Father, Meg, Jo, and Beth excused themselves. Amy slipped into her undergarments and then the new dress. She had never felt so pretty, and she could see from Marmee's satisfied look that the dress was a perfect fit.

"My friends will be so impressed," Amy said. "Aunt March's beautiful things, and ice cream, and now this dress. Oh, Marmee. I wish I could turn ten every single day."

"Once a year is enough, I think," Marmee said. "We all want this to be a day you'll remember forever, Amy, dearest."

"I will," Amy said. "May I wear the dress all day? I don't want to take it off, I love it so much."

"Of course," Marmee said. "I know you'll be careful in it."

Amy loved the feel of the new dress on her skin. Someday she was sure she'd go to balls every night of the week, wearing a different gown. But for now, this one dress was more precious than any princess's wardrobe.

Downstairs, she modeled the dress for Father, her sisters, and Hannah. They all agreed it was beautiful, and Amy couldn't remember ever having been so happy.

"My friends are coming at one o'clock," she reminded Marmee. "Things will be ready by then, won't they?"

"Absolutely," Marmee said. "Everyone is helping out to make sure they are."

"Keep me away from the china and the lace," Jo said. "For I'm sure to break one and rip the other."

"I'll handle the breakables," said Meg. "Jo, you can arrange the silver. You should be able to keep from damaging that."

"Look, Amy," Beth said. "Aunt March sent flowers from her greenhouse. I'll arrange them in a vase for the table."

"I'm off to town to get the ice cream," said Father. "Is there anything else we need while I'm at the store?"

"Just the ice cream," said Marmee. "Nothing else."

"May I go with you?" asked Amy. "I'd love a walk."

"She'd also love to see the selection of ice cream flavors," said Jo with a laugh. "And I don't blame you, Amy."

"I should be delighted to escort such a beautiful young lady," Father said. "Come, Amy. Let's stroll to the store and choose the ice cream that goes best with your cake."

Amy glowed with pleasure and excitement. Birthdays really were the best thing ever created.

CHAPTER 5

*A*my enjoyed the walk to town. Father was always so busy that it was rare to have private time with him. He asked her about her artwork, and Amy answered him seriously. She never took her dreams of being an artist lightly, and appreciated that Father respected her ambitions as much as he respected Jo's plans to be a writer.

They arrived at the new store that sold oysters and ice cream before they knew it, but before they could enter, Father spotted Mr. Marshall in the doorway of his bookshop.

"Mr. March! Mr. March!" Mr. Marshall called, waving a newspaper in his hand.

"I wonder what he wants," Father said. "I have no books on order."

"I suppose we should go over and find out," said Amy, though she was impatient to select the ice cream.

"I think we'd better," said Father. "Mr. Marshall seems quite agitated."

Amy followed her father to the bookstore. Mr. Marshall held the door open as they all entered the shop.

"Have you seen this?" he asked, pointing to the front page of the newspaper.

Amy frowned. Politics. Her father was deeply involved in the abolitionist movement, and Amy respected him for it, but she had hoped to avoid any mention of politics on her birthday.

"Father," she said, but he merely shook his head and commenced reading the paper.

"This is terrible news," he said, looking up.

"It had to happen," Mr. Marshall said. "We all knew it was just a matter of time once the Southern states began their move to secede."

"There's always the hope that war can be

avoided," Father said. "That people of good-will might come to their senses and work out a peaceable resolution instead."

"War?" Amy asked. "Are we at war?"

"We are," replied Father.

"Where?" Amy asked. She saw no signs of soldiers in the streets of Concord.

"Fort Sumter," Mr. Marshall said.

"Where's that?" Amy asked.

"In South Carolina," Father said. "When South Carolina seceded, back in December, they demanded that all federal lands be given to them. Of course the federal government refused. Our soldiers there moved to Fort Sumter, and yesterday Confederate troops fired on them. There seems to be no end in sight, and surely this will mean war."

"But we'll be safe, won't we, Father?" Amy asked. "There's no reason for anyone to fight a war here."

"I'm sure we'll be safe," said Father. "But safe does not mean unscarred, Amy. This war will change life as we know it in ways we cannot predict."

"Oh, Father," Amy said.

"The battles will spread like wildfire," Mr. Marshall predicted. "When the other Southern states hear what is happening in South Carolina, they'll open fire as well."

"But surely the war will end right away," Amy said. "The Southern states must realize they're in the wrong, and will return to the Union and give up slavery."

"That would be nice," said Mr. Marshall. "For otherwise I shall have to enlist. What will you do, Mr. March?"

"He'll stay at home with us!" Amy cried. "Father, you wouldn't ever leave us, would you?"

Father sighed. "It's a question I've been trying to answer since Mr. Lincoln's election," he said. "Amy, I can't tell you at this moment what my plans will be. But your mother and I have discussed all possibilities, and we both realize that in a time of war, none of us can be selfish."

"You wouldn't leave today," Amy said. "It's my birthday."

Father looked down at Amy. "Not today," he said. "Or tomorrow, either. But our soldiers will need ministering to, and that is probably how I can best help this country, which I love so much."

Amy breathed a sigh of relief. As long as Father wasn't planning to leave right away, there was a chance the war would end before there was any need for him to leave at all.

"Today's my birthday," she said to Mr. Marshall. "I'm ten now." Mr. Marshall had a rule that no one under ten could enter his store. Amy realized with a start that she had crossed his threshold without any objection from him. Either he knew she was ten, or this war had pushed all other issues aside.

"You'll have a birthday to remember," Mr. Marshall said. "Mr. March, Mr. Emerson was in the store a few minutes ago. He mentioned the possibility of our having a prayer service this afternoon. Would you be able to conduct it in your church?"

"Of course," Father said. "I think a day of quiet prayer might be the best thing for us all."

"But, Father!" Amy cried. "What about my party?"

"Oh," Father said. "This news has made me forget the reason for our walk. I'm sorry, Amy. It's suddenly very hard to think of celebration on a day such as this."

"You think I should cancel my party, don't you?" Amy asked.

Father shook his head. "That's not my decision to make. You're a child, Amy, and you shouldn't have to worry about such things."

But how was Amy not to worry? She knew she couldn't enjoy herself if soldiers were dying. "I'll tell my friends," she said. "You go home, Father, and tell Marmee and the others."

"We'll have a family party," Father said. "After the prayer service. I promise you, Amy."

"It's all right," Amy said. Father might say she was a child, but she knew better. Her childhood had ended the moment the first shot was fired in South Carolina.

CHAPTER 6

*A*my walked from one house to the next, telling her friends of the party's cancellation. Mary's house was closest, so Amy began with her.

"You're so brave," Mary said. "Sacrificing your party. I admire you so, Amy March."

Amy rather liked that reaction. Katy's was similar, although she spent more time complimenting Amy on her dress.

"I've heard all about the war," Jenny declared as Amy explained why she was calling. "Papa is simply thrilled. He says we'll make bundles of money selling supplies to the army, and that if the war lasts any length at all, we'll

161

be the richest family in New England. Imagine the parties I'll be able to give then!"

Amy thought about what Aunt March's response to that speech would be, even if Jenny's great-great-grandfather was Aunt March's grandmother's second cousin.

Susie took the news less well. "I don't see why you can't have a party," she said. "What difference does it make if some silly men get into a fight way off in South Carolina?"

Amy wasn't sure she knew the answer to that question. "It may not make a difference today," she replied. "But it will in the future. Father says the whole country will be changed because of this war."

"I'm sure I won't be changed one bit," Susie said. "Except I'll never accept an invitation from you again, Amy March. What manners to uninvite people on the very day of the party."

"I'll never do it again," Amy promised, since she doubted she'd ever have the courage to invite Jenny and Susie to her home another time.

The last stop was Rebecca's. Amy was stunned to see Rebecca's mother in tears when she opened the door.

"Is everything all right, Mrs. Winthrop?" Amy asked.

"My oldest boy, Harold," Mrs. Winthrop said. "He has run off to enlist in our army. My husband has gone to look for him, but I fear it will be too late."

"I'm so sorry," Amy said.

"I believe in the cause of our country," Mrs. Winthrop said. "And I know it's wrong for me to approve of other mothers' sons fighting the battle while I protect my own. But Harold is just eighteen, and I cannot bear to lose him."

Rebecca joined her mother in their front parlor. "I'm so sorry, Amy," she said. "But I can't leave Mother feeling this way, so I won't be able to attend your party."

"There is no party," Amy said, and for the first time she understood why the party had to be canceled and was glad she had come to that decision. "That's why I came. Father is holding a prayer service instead."

"We'll be there," Rebecca said. "Mother, you'll feel better if you go."

"I know," Mrs. Winthrop said, but she was crying so hard that Amy didn't know if she'd be able to leave her house. Amy said good-bye and began the short walk back to her own house.

"Oh, Amy!" Jo cried as Amy returned. "Father told us of your decision. I'm so proud of you."

"Thank you," Amy said. Words of praise from Jo were rare indeed. Amy only wished she could truly enjoy them.

"Father says he won't leave right away," Beth whispered. "But I'll hate it so if he leaves at all."

"He must do what he thinks is right," Jo said. "I only wish I could go too. It's so blasted useless being a girl."

"There is no excuse for bad language," Meg said. "And you shouldn't think of yourself as useless. I'm sure there will be many things we'll be able to do to help our soldiers in the fight ahead."

"Marmee will know what we can do," Beth said. "Marmee always knows."

But when Marmee joined them in the parlor, she didn't look like one who knew. Amy could see that Marmee had been crying. The very sight of Marmee with reddened eyes terrified her.

"Come here, Amy," Marmee said. Amy did as she was told. "I cannot tell you how proud I am of you," Marmee continued. "And how grateful to you I am. I don't think I could have pretended to enjoy myself at your party, with my heart so saddened."

"It will be all right, Marmee," Jo said. "We'll win this war, and free the slaves, and the world will be a better place."

"I'm sure you're right," Marmee replied. "God will hear our prayers and put an end to the suffering of slaves and lead our country on the path of righteousness. But I can't help fearing the loss that will be endured until a time of peace and justice is reached."

"We'll get through it together," Meg said. "And we'll be the better for our sacrifices."

Marmee nodded. "So much has gone on this morning, we've hardly had a chance to eat," she said. "And missing our meals will not shorten this war any. How about an early lunch, girls, and then we'll attend the prayer service together."

"Marmee?" Amy asked.

"Yes, dearest?"

"Might we have my birthday cake?" Amy asked.

Marmee smiled. "Hannah would never forgive us if we didn't," she said. "And it will remind all of us that no matter how bitter the times, there is sweetness if we take the time to look for it. Come, girls. Let's eat our meal and enjoy Amy's cake."

Somehow Marmee convinced Father and Hannah to join them. There was little conversation, but it comforted Amy to be surrounded by those she loved. She was glad, as Marmee had been, that she didn't have to pretend to be enjoying herself just to satisfy her party guests.

"It's time for the cake now," Jo said. "Hannah, it looks delicious."

"It may look that way, but there's danger in it," Hannah answered. "Watch when you bite, for fear of what you might find."

"Let Amy do the slicing," Meg said. "It is her birthday, after all."

Amy took the beautiful silver cake slicer that Aunt March had sent for the day. She cut pieces of cake for each of her sisters, her parents, Hannah, and herself.

"I've bitten into something!" Meg cried. "It's the ring."

"That means you'll marry," Amy said.

"I should hope so," said Meg. "I wonder if it will be a soldier."

"I pray the war won't last that long," said Marmee.

"I've something in my slice too," said Beth. "Oh, dear. It's the thimble. Does that mean I'll marry a tailor?"

"No, it means you'll never marry at all," Amy said. "Although I'm sure that won't be true in your case, Beth."

"I have the button," Jo said. "Perhaps I'm the one who'll marry the tailor!"

"A button means you'll always be poor," said Amy.

"A fine cake this is!" Jo said. "Beth, I think you and I should demand new slices."

Amy cut into her slice and found the coin.

"Don't tell me," Jo said. "That means you'll be rich."

"I'm afraid so," Amy said with a laugh.

"It's good that one of us will," Jo said. "And it might as well be you, Amy. Just remember your poor sisters once you come into your fortune."

But Amy knew, looking at her family, that she could never have a greater fortune than the love she felt at that moment. Whatever the future might hold, she was already rich in every way that mattered.

PORTRAITS OF LITTLE WOMEN RECIPES

CHOCOLATE FUDGE CAKE

Many people say a cake isn't a cake unless it's chocolate. Here's one that's sure to make your mouth water.

INGREDIENTS
10 ounces semisweet chocolate
½ pound (2 sticks) unsalted butter
3 eggs plus 2 egg yolks
¼ cup granulated sugar
walnut halves for topping, about 12
powdered sugar for topping

NOTE: This cake is best when made a day in advance. Also, make sure a grown-up helps you.

1. Preheat oven to 350 degrees. Grease and flour an 8-inch round cake pan.
2. Melt chocolate and butter over hot water. (Chocolate and butter go into a small pot that you place in a larger pot filled with water; bring water to a gentle boil on stove.)
3. Remove from heat and add eggs and egg yolks, one at a time, blending well after each addition.
4. Stir in granulated sugar.
5. Pour chocolate mixture into greased pan.
6. Bake about 30 minutes. Center of cake should be soft.
7. Cool at room temperature, then refrigerate overnight.
8. Finish off with a dusting of powdered sugar. Decorate edges with evenly spaced walnut halves all around.

Makes about 12 servings.

ALMOND CAKE

*The almonds make every bite of this cake
absolutely scrumptious.*

INGREDIENTS

1½ cups sliced almonds (plus extra for
  decoration)
¼ cup potato starch
1 tablespoon unsalted butter
1 tablespoon vegetable oil
¾ cup granulated sugar
1 teaspoon vanilla extract
3 egg yolks
2 tablespoons milk
5 egg whites
powdered sugar for topping

NOTE: Make sure a grown-up helps you.

1. Preheat oven to 325 degrees. Grease and flour an 8-inch round cake pan.
2. Finely chop almonds. Place them in a large bowl and add potato starch, butter, oil, sugar (all but 2 tablespoons), vanilla, egg yolks, and milk. Mix until smooth.
3. In another bowl, beat egg whites until firm, then add remaining 2 tablespoons of granulated sugar and beat.
4. Fold egg white mixture into almond mixture and pour into greased cake pan.
5. Bake for 35 minutes, or until set. Cool at room temperature.
6. Decorate outer edge of cake with extra almonds, then sprinkle top with powdered sugar.

Makes 8 to 10 servings.

WALNUT CARROT CAKE

You'll want more than one piece of this tasty, light carrot cake.

INGREDIENTS
2 cups flour
2 teaspoons ground cinnamon
1 teaspoon baking powder
$1/4$ teaspoon salt
$2/3$ cup butter
1 cup sugar
3 eggs
$2/3$ cup milk
3 medium carrots, grated
$1/2$ cup chopped walnuts

Optional toppings:
 $^1/_4$ cup chopped walnuts and 2 tablespoons
 brown sugar, *or* powdered sugar

NOTE: Make sure a grown-up helps you.

1. Preheat oven to 350 degrees. Grease and
   flour an 8-inch round cake pan.
2. In a medium bowl, mix together flour,
   cinnamon, baking powder, and salt.
3. In a large bowl, beat together butter and
   sugar until light and fluffy. Add eggs and
   beat well.
4. Alternate adding flour mixture and milk,
   beating well each time.
5. Stir in carrots and walnuts.
6. Pour into greased cake pan and bake for
   about 45 minutes. Cool at room temperature.
7. Place cake on serving plate and either
   sprinkle top with cup chopped walnuts and
   2 tablespoons brown sugar mixed together,
   or dust with powdered sugar.

   Makes 10 to 12 servings.

POPPY SEED CAKE

The airy texture of this cake guarantees that you'll have room for more than one slice!

INGREDIENTS
2 cups flour
2 teaspoons baking powder
pinch of salt
2/3 cup milk
1 1/2 cups sugar
4 eggs, separated
2/3 cup melted butter
1 teaspoon vanilla
2/3 cup poppy seeds
ice cream as an accompaniment (optional)

NOTE: Make sure a grown-up helps you.

1. Preheat oven to 350 degrees. Grease and flour an 8-inch round cake pan.
2. In a small bowl, combine flour, baking powder, and salt.
3. In a large bowl, combine milk, sugar, egg yolks, melted butter, vanilla, and poppy seeds. Beat well.
4. Add dry ingredients and beat.
5. Beat egg whites until stiff and fold into cake mixture.
6. Bake for 40 minutes. Cool at room temperature.

Serve with ice cream if you wish. Makes about 10 servings.

ABOUT THE AUTHOR OF
PORTRAITS OF LITTLE WOMEN

SUSAN BETH PFEFFER is the author of both middle-grade and young adult fiction. Her middle-grade novels include *Nobody's Daughter* and its companion, *Justice for Emily*. Her highly praised *The Year Without Michael* is an ALA Best Book for Young Adults, an ALA YALSA Best of the Best, and a *Publishers Weekly* Best Book of the Year. Her novels for young adults include *Twice Taken, Most Precious Blood, About David,* and *Family of Strangers*. Susan Beth Pfeffer lives in Middletown, New York.

A WORD ABOUT
LOUISA MAY ALCOTT

LOUISA MAY ALCOTT was born in 1832 in Germantown, Pennsylvania, and grew up in the Boston-Concord area of Massachusetts. She received her early education from her father, Bronson Alcott, a renowned educator and writer, who eventually left teaching to study philosophy. To supplement the family income, Louisa worked as a teacher, a household servant, and a seamstress, and she wrote stories as well as poems for newspapers and magazines. In 1868 she published the first volume of *Little Women,* a novel about four sisters growing up in a small New England town during the Civil War. The immediate success of *Little Women* made Louisa May Alcott a celebrated writer, and the novel remains one of today's best-loved books. Alcott wrote until her death in 1888.